Love by the Master

"This is such an inspiring story that will put a smile on your face and love in your heart. It tells how you can have a difficult life with one problem after another, but when you let God into your life, you can see things differently. The love of God in one woman's life touches and changes so many people. I loved this story and pray that I can be more like Leah." —Annita

"Vicki did an amazing job on this book… Once I started reading, I didn't want to put it down! If you are having a difficult time in your life, pick up her book and it will lift you up and inspire you… Love you, Vicki… I am ready for a sequel!!!" —Kathy

Praise for Vicki Irwin's A Journey for Rebecca

"I have to say this is one of the best written book I have read in many months. It deals with heartache, loss, and then redemption. The characters are a very varied group of people who work together for the good of all." —Irma Gray

"I truly loved "A Journey for Rebecca" and enjoyed following along with her story. I found myself getting sucked into the story and the characters were very engaging and endearing. Mrs. Irwin weaves a bittersweet story about how we all need to trust in God for He alone knows our path even if there is pain getting to where we need to be." —Rebecca Johnston

"I didn't even realize how captivated I was with the main character until I caught myself shedding a tear! A sweet and wholesome story and I'd like to read more." —Carolyne Greene

"You will be engrossed from the beginning of 'A Journey for Rebecca'. A treat to look into her life as she touches so many. We do need more Rebecca's in the world. I couldn't put it down." —KGA

"I am a voracious reader but once I discovered Kindle books 10 years ago, I never picked up an actual hardcover or paperback book again.….until I read "A JOURNEY FOR REBECCA." Thus, I read a few pages, thinking if I liked it I would order it as an eBook. This actual book just drew me into the story until I just read the entire book. The lead character was very inspiring in her staunch belief in God and praying about everything, the way she treated everyone and ……I JUST LOVE THIS AUTHOR. She truly is an inspiration and her faith shines forth through her book." —Bonnie Winchester

"You'll enjoy this beautifully written story with highs, lows, and surprises. The ending is multi-layered and wraps up loose ends with grace notes! Can't wait for the next book from Vicki McBee Irwin." —Thomas Gilmore

Love by the Master

By

Vicki McBee Irwin

Knoxville, Tennessee, USA
crippledbeaglepublishing.com

Cover design by Maria Loysa-Bel Nueve - de los Angeles

Follow Vicki Lynn McBee-Irwin on Facebook

Scriptures marked NIV are taken from the NEW INTERNATIONAL VERSION (NIV): Scripture taken from THE HOLY BIBLE, NEW INTERNATIONAL VERSION ®. Copyright© 1973, 1978, 1984, 2011 by Biblica, Inc.™. Used by permission of Zondervan.

Paperback ISBNs 978-1-958533-95-6, 978-1-958533-97-0
Hardcover ISBN 978-1-958533-96-3, 978-1-958533-98-7
Library of Congress Control Number: 2024912116

Printed in the United States of America

I want to thank our dear heavenly Father for giving me the stories that I have written. He has blessed me with the writing of a third book. Each book has brought me so much joy and has been a blessing. I pray that each of these books will bless you and if you or someone you know are going through similar situations, that in some way it will lift you up.

Blessings to all
Vicki Irwin

Many thanks to my wonderful editor Linda Albert. You are a jewel. Thank you for all your help, I really appreciate you, and to my wonderful publisher Jody Dyer. I know this year has been a hard year for you, yet you were always available when I called. You ladies made all this possible for me. Blessing to you both.

One

ooking at her watch, it was only seven-thirty. Liz Barnett thought, I still have some time to catch up on some paperwork that I have put off doing. As she walked in the office, she noticed the picture hanging behind the desk was tilted a little. Reaching up to straighten it, she took her finger and traced over the house in the picture. Oh, the memories that home held.

When she purchased the house, she remembered thinking this was way more than she needed, but the price was right, and she could not pass it up. Little did she know what was ahead for her. Letting her mind wander back to how things all started, she sat down in the chair at the desk and stared at the picture.

Her parents were childhood sweethearts. Not only that, but her dad's brother was dating her mom's sister. The two couples did everything together. A few years after they graduated, the two couples had a double wedding. They even bought a home next door to each other. Her dad and uncle opened an Auto Parts store together and called it Barnett's Auto Parts Store. Two years later, Liz's mom and her aunt became pregnant. On June 20, Liz was born to Ryan and Dana Barnett. On June 22, Millie was born to Roy and Debbie Barnett. It was only natural that the two girls grew up as sisters instead of cousins. Like their parents, they did everything together. They went to church and school and even participated in the same sports. Liz had dark brown hair and eyes. Millie had light brown hair and dark brown eyes. They were the same height and weight. Both girls in the summer always had a golden tan. Almost everyone who saw them thought they were twins or at least sisters.

Soon it was time to graduate from high school and go to college. Liz went to Yale University. Her goal was to be an attorney. Millie went to Johns Hopkins to study nursing with the potential of going on to be a physician's assistant.

They talked every night while in college. One year it was close to Thanksgiving, and the girls had promised to come in for the holiday. They were almost four years into college. Liz knew she had several more years to go and Millie was close to becoming a registered nurse. At this point, she was not sure if she wanted to go on to further pursue the medical field.

Liz made it home first and was anxiously waiting for Millie to arrive. The families were getting ready to sit down to eat when Millie walked in. Everyone was so excited to see her when a guy appeared behind her. Everyone stopped talking and looked at him.

Millie spoke up, "This is my boyfriend, Alex Sailor."

Debbie held out her hand and said, "Hello, I'm Millie's mom.

The room had become cold, and it felt like a dark cloud had entered in. Then Debbie proceeded to introduce everyone.

Millie and Alex took a seat next to Liz. Millie was chatting away, but everyone else struggled to say anything. Although Alex would smile at you, something about him didn't seem right, but the family did the best they could to make the meal enjoyable.

After lunch, Liz helped clean up, then decided to go for a walk. As many times as she had talked to Millie on the phone, not once had she said anything about a boyfriend. Something about him bothered Liz. He seemed polite, yet she couldn't put her finger on it. What was it?

Liz had just found a park bench to sit on, when she heard Millie call her name. Walking up to Liz, Millie asked, "What's wrong? You don't seem yourself? In fact, the whole family is acting weird."

"Millie, we have talked nearly every night since we left for college, and not once have you ever mentioned a guy, and then, you show up today with a guy you say is your boyfriend! What is this all about?"

"Liz, you never mentioned liking a guy and I didn't want you to feel bad, that I had a boyfriend, and you didn't."

"Millie, how long have you known Alex?"

"Oh, about two months. He is really a great guy. If you would give him a chance Liz, I know you would like him too. He has big plans for his future."

"I'm sorry, Millie, but something about him isn't right and I think the rest of the family feels the same way. Before you say anything, no, I haven't been talking to anyone. I'm going by the expression on their faces and the fact that lunch was such a strain. When he walked in, it was as if evil forces walked in."

"Liz, this isn't like you to judge people. We were always taught to pray, listen to our heart, and walk by faith. Is this what they are teaching you in law school? If anything, I thought sure you would be supportive of me."

"I'm sorry, Millie. Have you talked to your mom?"

"No. Alex went outside to look around and I went looking for you. Liz, I need you on my side. I love Alex and he loves me."

"Please, Millie, take it slow with Alex. You haven't known him long enough to know if you really are in love. Give this sometime, please."

"I know you're just jealous because you didn't bring a guy home first. Maybe if you didn't spend so much time with your nose in those law books, you might find someone."

"No, I'm not jealous of you at all. I am very concerned. Remember, he's not the only guy around. Take some time and look around, weigh out your options."

"Thanks, Liz. The one person I knew I could count on just let me down."

Millie turned and walked away. Liz bowed her head and prayed for Millie. She knew something wasn't right. By the time Liz had got back home, Millie and Alex had left to go back to Johns Hopkins. Dana was trying to comfort Debbie and Roy was around back talking to Ryan.

As soon as Debbie saw Liz, she asked, "Did you talked to Millie?"

"I'm sorry Aunt Debbie, but nothing I said did any good." Knowing this was not what her aunt wanted to hear, Liz went home and went straight to her bedroom. Lying across the bed, looking up at the ceiling, Liz wondered, "What was it about Alex that the family was so concerned about?"

Two

*J*ust before Christmas, Liz's mom, Dana, called to let her know that Millie had dropped out of school and had married Alex. Debbie and Roy were beside themselves. Debbie and Dana had visions of a big wedding for the girls. With this news, Debbie didn't want anything to do with Christmas, so the four had decided to take a trip instead of staying home.

Dana asked Liz, "We have decided to go out to Colorado to do some skiing. Would you like to come with us?"

"No, Mom if it's alright, I need to stay here and do some studying. I appreciate the offer; besides, you know me. Always striving to make top score on any test."

Hanging up the phone, Liz thought, ever since Thanksgiving, Millie had not called her, nor had she answered or returned any of her calls. Now this. Liz couldn't believe Millie would up and quit school, only to go off and marry a guy she barely knew. Why?

Bowing her head, with tears in her eyes, Liz tried to pray. So many thoughts were going through her mind, she wanted to pray for what was best for the family, but she didn't know what to pray. Her roommate, Glenda Felty, walked in, put her hand on Liz's arm, and asked, "Need an extra prayer partner?"

"Yes, my family needs prayers. I never thought something like this would happen to us."

Glenda said, "If you want to share your heartache, I'm here. If not, I'll pray anyway, for God knows what's on your heart. We must pray believing and have faith in those prayers."

"Glenda, I don't mind sharing. I have told you a lot about my cousin Millie. Well, the one thing that the family didn't want to happen has happened. Millie quit school and married Alex Sailor."

"Oh, Liz, I am so sorry. From what you have told me, this can't be good. How are Millie's parents taking this?"

"Not good. Aunt Debbie doesn't want to be home for Christmas, so she, Uncle Roy and my parents are going skiing in Colorado. Mom called and asked if I would like to join them, but I told her no. With me being there, I feel it would only hurt Aunt Debbie and Uncle Roy more. Besides, I have plenty of reading to do to keep me busy."

"Liz, why don't you come home with me for Christmas? Have you ever been to Raleigh, North Carolina?"

"No, can't say I have."

"Please come home with me and I can show you around. It will help take your mind off things. If you stay here, you will only sit here and worry about Millie. What do you say?"

"You know Glenda, I think I'll take you up on your offer. You have been the best roommate anyone could want. I'm sure God brought us together for a reason."

"Great, I'll let my parents know. Now, we need to get back to praying for your family."

With heads bowed, the girls held hands and prayed.

The trip to Raleigh was wonderful. Glenda's dad was a Baptist preacher, and her mom was a housewife. When they were ready to go back to Yale, Mr. Felty hug Glenda and whispered something to her, then he hugged, Liz and whispered, "Liz, no matter what you do, always live by faith. Your faith will carry you through."

She had never forgotten those kind words. They had become very dear to her, and how many times she had repeated those words.

Finally, the day had come that Liz and Glenda made it through law school. Next was the bar exam, which would be in three months. Liz had asked her parents to hold off on a party until she knew for sure she had passed the bar. While at home studying, Liz would occasionally try to call Millie. From time to time, Millie would send her mom, Debbie, a short text, but would never reply to a text sent to her. Millie's text would say, "Doing good. Love you." This of course would break her Aunt Debbie's heart. A million things would go through her mind about Millie. She always felt Millie was hiding something.

On the day of the bar exam, Liz was so delighted to see Glenda. They had so much to catch up on, but first the test.

After the test, the two talked almost non-stop the next day. They had become very close friends, and especially prayer partners.

Six weeks later, Liz had received the letter she had been waiting so anxiously for. Before opening it, once again she knelt to pray, remembering Mr. Felty's words. Then she decided to call Glenda to see if she had received her letter. She had and so they opened their letters at the same time.

Glenda let out a scream. She had made the third highest score from the bar exam. Liz made the fourth highest score and was just as happy. Together they prayer over the phone to give God the glory.

How Liz wished she could share this news with Millie.

Liz had received several calls from different law firms asking her to consider employment with their company. She finally decided on one in Nashville so she could be close to her family. The pay was not as much as others had offered, but family meant more to her than the money.

Glenda had been offered a position in Raleigh, which was close to her family. She had been offered other jobs with better pay, but like Liz, family came first.

Liz put on the prayer list at church that she was looking for a house to purchase, and if anyone knew of one, please let her know. The very next Sunday, a couple came up to her and said they were being transferred and were going to sell their house. It wasn't on the market yet and they asked Liz to come take a look.

It was a much larger house than Liz needed, but the price was one she could not pass up. Once she moved in, Liz's parents, Ryan and Dana came by to see her new home. Dana suggested she fix the house up, rent one side and live in the other. Not sure if this was what she wanted to do, again she went to her church with her concern and asked they pray with her on making a good decision.

A few weeks later, after Liz got home from work, she heard a knock at her door. Opening it, she gasped. They're stood Millie. She had been beaten and could hardly walk. Liz helped her inside, to the closest chair.

"Millie, sit still for a minute and then I'll help you to the bedroom if you think you can make it," Liz said.

Millie groaned and asked for a drink. Liz went to the kitchen for a glass of water and when she returned, Millie had slump over. Not sure what to do, she finally roused Millie enough to help her to the bedroom. Taking a cloth and pan of water, Liz began trying to wash Millie's face. Deep down inside, she knew Alex was responsible for this. After a couple of hours, Millie began to come around. When she saw Liz, she began to cry.

"Oh, Liz, I have made such a mess of my life. I should have listened to you and my parents. But I gave everything up for Alex, he made so many promises and I fell for every one of them. I need help, I can't go back, I can't take his beatings anymore. I'm afraid he will kill me."

"Millie, don't you worry, I won't let Alex near you again. I promise."

"Liz, I know you are an attorney, but I'm afraid when you are not looking, he will come after me. You don't understand him like I do. Once he gets to drinking and gets something on his mind, nothing stops him. I don't want you to go through what I have gone through."

"Millie, I take it this is not your first beating?" asked Liz.

"No. This is one of the reasons I don't come around. I usually have a mark or two on me and I didn't want anyone to see me like that. The nurses I work with have begged me to leave him. Today, I came home from work late, I had to stay over because of an emergency at the hospital. On my way home, I completely forgot to stop and pick up his laundry at the cleaners and I also didn't pick up his beer at the store. When he came home, dinner was late, which didn't sit well, and I overcooked it. When he asked about his laundry, the expression on my face let him know I didn't pick it up. That was a no-no, then when he opened the refrigerator and saw no beer, he asked if I forgot to pick his beer up also. I tried to explain about my day, but that was no excuse in his eyes. He slammed the refrigerator door and came at me. Accused me of not being responsible and asked what kind of a woman I was. Could I not remember to do little things that he asked of me. Then he hit me in the face and all I felt after that was pain in so many areas of my body."

"Millie, lay still and just relax for a few minutes. I need to make some phone calls. Don't worry, I'm not calling your parents, the police or anyone like that. I'm going to call a friend who can help."

Liz went to her makeshift desk and called Glenda Felty and explained the reason for her phone call. Glenda was more than happy to help. Liz called work and stated she was taking a few days off, then went and packed an overnight bag. When she went back to Millie to explain they were taking a trip to North Carolina, Millie told Liz she had packed some suitcases, and they were at the front door.

"You see Liz, I was prepared for the next time Alex gave me a beating. I knew it was coming, so I had been packing a few things a little at a time. It made getting away quicker."

So, Liz loaded up Millie's suitcases and her overnight bag and headed to Raleigh, North Carolina. Glenda had a home set up for abusive women. She took in women from neighboring states and sent the women there in Raleigh that needed a safe place to other states.

When Liz and Millie arrived, Glenda had a room all set up for Millie. Liz found an empty bed to rest on for a few hours before heading back to Nashville. Before leaving, Glenda and Liz talked. Glenda explained why she started this home and there was a great need for homes like hers in other states. A client had come to her one day in need of a safe place to go, and the idea came to her to open a home for abused women. So, this is how the "House of Blessings" was born. Liz was inspired by what Glenda had done, so Glenda gave Liz information on how she went about getting started.

The drive back to Nashville gave Liz plenty of time to think and pray. She had a big home, and she could start a home for abused women. She wondered how many more women needed a safe place to go.

As she drove down the road, Liz began to pray.

"Dear Father in Heaven, I believe each of us have been gifted a great purpose. I pray that I can help others to be encouraged, to fulfill their purpose and Your will for their lives. May Your Holy Spirit use me to speak life into them, share ideas, to affirm, and keep accountable. Whether it be a stranger in need or a family member, whoever You place in my life, help me to be a blessing. Give me the courage to share and give me the wisdom to share. Help me to point them toward You. Amen."

That Sunday, she went before her church with what she wanted to do, asking the church for prayers and support. By that Wednesday, church members were donating furniture they no longer needed, and people that were retired wanted to help. Soon her house was full of furniture and walls in the house were being moved to make the house more feasible. Not sure what to name her home, she decided to wait till women started coming in.

Liz didn't have to wait long. While at work one day, a lady called and said she had heard about the safe house and asked what she needed to do to stay there. Liz met her and took her to her house. When the women at the church found out, two came over to stay so Liz could go back to work. One was a retired registered nurse; the other had been a bookkeeper for a corporation for years.

In three months' time Liz was running out of room. Like Glenda had said, "Don't keep locals, only keep women from other states." She soon had contact with different agencies all over, and the need was much greater than what she had anticipated.

Going before the church again, Liz explained she was out of room and didn't want to turn anyone away. Again, she was looking for a bigger place to go. The next day, an older couple of the church called and asked to stop by to see Liz. When they showed up at her office, she was not expecting to hear what they had to say.

They owned Master's clothing store in downtown Nashville, which was very well known. It was a three-story building, in great shape, and in a good location. They also had a store in Colorado, Kentucky, and Maine, with another store opening in Florida in about two months. Master's Department Store had been in the family for five generations. Each of Mr. and Mrs. Master's children ran the stores in the other states. Due to their health, they were planning on closing the one in Nashville and moving to Florida. They lived upstairs at the department store, and it had a full basement. The building would soon be vacant and needed someone to love and care for it.

Liz had shopped at Master's many times and loved the place. She could only imagine what they would be asking for the building. It was in a very good location, everything you could want. The building even had security cameras, alarm system, and could handle setting up many individuals rooms.

Looking at them both, Liz smiled, took a deep breath, and said, "How much are you asking for your store? You know you are in a great location, and everyone loves Master's. If you close, what will the people around here do?"

Mr. Master sat back in his chair, looking at Liz. "Young lady, we are here to make you an offer that you can't afford to pass up. We realize you will need to renovate the inside to make it work for you, and we have taken everything into consideration that we could think of. As you know, I'm sure, Gloria and I want for nothing. God has blessed us over the years, not only with a wonderful business, but with five wonderful children. Each of our stores has been blessed over and over. We put a conference call in to our children and explained some things to them. They agreed, and we had prayer over the phone. Can't explain the peace we had, and we knew this was the right thing to do. Ms. Liz, we are giving you Master's to turn it into a shelter for abused women and children. Like I said, we realize the insides will have to be renovated to accommodate your needs. We will be having a closeout sell very soon, and all the money taken in at that sale will go for your renovation."

Liz sat in her chair unable to move. Was she hearing Bill Master correctly? She had prayed and even asked the church to help her pray, but she had no idea of something like this.

Gloria leaned over the desk and placed her hand on Liz's. "Child, are you alright? You are as pale as a ghost."

Still trying to wrap her mind around what she had just heard, Liz finally spoke. "Let me make sure I'm hearing you correctly. You are giving Master's store to me to turn into a shelter for abused women and children?"

Bill Master smiled. "Don't forget all the money from the closeout sale goes for renovation."

Still in a state of shock, Liz just sat there. Then tears started streaming down her face. It was as if she was frozen in her chair.

Gloria went around the desk and gave Liz a hug. "God is so good, Liz. All we must do is asked and believe in Him. You needed a building and we needed to give one away."

Liz finally was able to speak. "God provided the first house for me. At first, I didn't understand why, but soon I realize what that house could become. Now this. How can I ever repay you? Saying 'Thank you' just doesn't seem enough."

Gloria gave Liz another hug and said, "Liz, you went off to law school, and look at you. You are a fine lawyer. Family meant more to you than moving away where you could make the big bucks. Everything you do, you put your whole heart into. You rely on God and your church, and it shows. Your love for people is extraordinary. Our family wants to help, and this is our way of helping, not only you but those that knock on your door. You turn no one away. Just like Jesus, it doesn't matter who you are, He loves you and wants to help you. We see Jesus in you."

Liz could not control her tears. "I pray I can live up to being the person you think I am. I feel I fall so short in so many ways. I do love people and want to help any way I can. Being an attorney, sometimes I must be so stern and not let my heart get in the way. I struggle so. Again, thank you from the bottom of my heart and thank you in advance for every woman that walks through that door for help."

Bill Master asked Liz if she would mind if they had prayer. They stood in a circle, holding hands, while Bill Master prayed. Liz could still see that day in her mind as if it was yesterday. She could feel tears rolling down her cheek. What a special day that was and look at the place now.

Just like the Masters, she lived upstairs. God had allowed so many wonderful things to come her way. Every day, she thanked God and prayed that whoever came through the door would be blessed. She also felt it only right to keep the name Master on the building, so she called her place, 'Love by the Master,' for the name served a two-fold meaning. The family named Master gave her the building, her heavenly Master brought it all together, and it was all in love.

As Liz looked around, her eyes went back to the picture of her first home. Who would have ever thought she would have gone from that house to this place? That picture meant so much to her, for that is where it all started.

Lost in her thoughts, a knock at the door startled Liz. She turned to see who her visitor could be, but no one came in although the door was unlocked. Since there was only one knock, Liz speculated that a bird or perhaps a rock had bounced off the door. Deciding to try to get back on track and get some paperwork done, Liz turned in her seat. An uneasy feeling came over her, so she went to the door, seeing no one till she looked down. There lay a young girl, beaten so badly she could not move. Liz immediately went inside, pressed the alarm button for help, then returned to the young girl.

Jana Stokes, Nina Pearson, and Gill Macon came to the door. When they saw the young girl, they all three gasped. Nina went back in to call an ambulance.

They were not sure if they should move the girl, who was seriously bruised and bleeding. You could slightly hear her moan. Jana went to get some towels with ice to place on the girl's face to help with some of the swelling. The girl was curled up in a fetal position and never moved. Liz reached out to touch her hand and began praying. Never had she seen anyone beaten so badly.

Soon the ambulance arrived and the two EMTs carefully assessed the situation for the best possible way to assist the patient. Slowly they placed her on the stretcher, only for the girl to moan in much pain. They rushed her to Tristar Skyline Medical Hospital, for they were a recognized trauma hospital. The EMTs were not sure if the girl would survive due to the severity of her injuries. Liz followed in her car.

In the emergency room, they immediately started treating the patient. Colleen Rivers, a friend of Liz's, was the registered nurse on duty. After about thirty minutes, Colleen came out to talk to Liz.

"Liz, do you know this girl?" Colleen asked.

"No, someone dumped her off at my door and left. She was beaten so badly it's hard to tell who she is."

Colleen took a deep breath and looked at Liz. "We are prepping her for surgery. She has some broken bones, dislocated shoulder and hip, punctured lung, bruises all over her body. She is unconscious, but we must do surgery to stop some bleeding. Whoever did this to her must have been drunk or totally out of their mind. I have been a nurse for twenty years and never have I ever seen someone beaten as badly as she is."

"Colleen, since we don't know anything about her, would you keep me informed on her condition?" I'll be waiting out here during her surgery, praying. Whoever did this at least had the good sense to drop her off at my door. That child is certainly in the Master's hands."

Colleen reached out to hug Liz. "That poor child needs someone, and I can't think of anyone better than you. I'll let you know as soon as I can. Also, call the church and let them know an urgent unspoken request is needed, for that child needs every prayer anyone can spare. There is a room near the surgery area where you can wait and have more privacy. By the way, the police have been notified and will be looking for you to get all the answers they can. I think they are at your place now talking to your workers."

"Thanks Colleen. I'll be praying till I hear from you."

Three

As Liz sat waiting for news on the young girl, she bowed her head and began to pray.

"Dear heavenly Father, I bow before you on behalf of that precious child that was placed at my door. I know nothing about her, but I know You do. Thank You that she was not left in a ditch or dropped off on the side of the road somewhere. Loving Father, I ask You to touch her now with Your healing hands, for I believe that Your will for her is to be healed in mind, body, soul, and spirit. Cover her with the most precious blood of Your son, our Lord Jesus Christ. From the top of her head to the soles of her feet, heal her. Open any blocked arteries or veins and rebuild and replenish any damage areas. Remove all inflammation and cleanse any infection. By the power of Jesus' precious blood, let the fire of Your healing love pass through her entire body to heal and make new. Also, Lord, touch her mind and her emotions, even the deepest depth of her heart. Saturate her entire being with Your presence, Your love, joy, and peace. Fill her with Your Holy Spirit so that her life will bring glory and honor to Your Holy name. Amen."

Liz sat in the room for nine hours. She had called work to let them know where she was and she also called the house to let

Jana, Nina, and Gill know what was going on and to be in prayer. The prayer line at church was also notified, for Liz knew this poor child needed lots of prayer. The rest of the time, she prayed to herself. Finally, Colleen came out and sat beside Liz.

Looking at Liz, Colleen shook her head. "The young lady is in worse shape than what we thought. She is facing more surgery if she survives the next twenty-four hours. Whoever did this to her must have kept beating her even after she became unconscious. I can't imagine the pain she went through, but at least they had the good sense to drop her off at your door."

"Colleen, is it possible for me to see her? I want to pray over her again. I've been praying, but I want to lay hands on her. Let her know God is with her."

"I will be her nurse for the night. Once I get her settled in a unit, I'll let you in for a few minutes. She is not going to know anyone is there, but like you, I do believe in prayer, and I can't deny you that."

"Thank you, Colleen. I'll send out a text to everyone that she is in ICU and prayer is very urgent. I don't guess you have had any news on who she is or how old?"

"Liz, we have no idea who she is or where she came from. As for her age, I'm guessing around fourteen or fifteen. It could be several days or even weeks before she can talk and tell us anything. It all depends on when she can wake up. I need to get back to her. Stay here and I'll come get you as soon as I can."

Sitting back down in the chair, Liz started sending out texts to update those praying on the young girl's condition. When she finished, she knelt to pray once more. As she prayed, she felt a light breeze come over her. Liz knew God was with her and He was with that young girl also. She made up her mind to be there for the girl every day and do her best to find out who did this to her. Even if this girl had done something wrong, no one deserved this kind of punishment.

Soon, Colleen opened the door. "Liz, if you will follow me, you can see the young girl, but only for a few minutes. Let me say, she is hooked up to a lot of things. We are trying to keep her alive and we are monitoring her constantly. I just want you to be prepared for what you're about to see."

They stepped off the elevator and walked down a long hall, stopping next to the nurse's desk. Across from that was a large glass window, and behind that window was the young girl, with everything you could imagine hooked up to her. Her face didn't even look like a face, it was so swollen, bruised, and bloody. Tears streamed down Liz's face.

"Oh, dear God, please be with that child. Hold her Lord, in your loving arms. She can't reach out to you, but you can reach out to her. Ease her pain, heal her body."

"Liz, do you still want to go in?" Colleen asked.

"Yes, yes, I do. I'm sorry. I know you tried to prepare me, but still, seeing her breaks my heart."

"I know. I'm a nurse and this has been hard for me. I'll give you ten minutes alone with her. Don't try to ask her any questions. Just talk to her and let her know you are here for her."

Liz walked in, stood by the young girl's bed, and reached over to touch her arm to pray. When she did, again, a light breeze came blowing by. Looking at the child, Liz said, "I know you may not be aware of this, but God is here with you. He is going to heal you and make you strong. We suffer at times and don't know why, but God knows. He has a plan for you. My name is Liz, and we are going to be friends, very special friends." Then Liz prayed.

"Dear Heavenly Father, God, Your Word says the prayer of faith shall heal the sick. We come to You today in faith asking that You heal this child. I ask that You not only bring healing, but comfort and peace to her body. Calm her fears and let her experience Your healing power of Your love. May she find strength each day to battle the physical challenges. Restore her health, soothe her pain and any fear she may have. Father, I know You are here in our midst, and I thank You. Thank You, Dear Lord. Amen."

Liz could not keep back the tears for the girl. She was determined to find out who did this and why. No one deserved this kind of treatment.

Colleen opened the door, "Liz, time is up. I know you want to stay, but I am already bending the rules letting you in here to see her."

"Colleen, is it possible that I can drop by each morning and in the evening to pray over her? Deep in my heart, I feel the need to do this."

"Liz, you can only stay long enough to pray over her. If things take a turn for the worse, you will have to pray out in the hall. I promise, if any changes, I will call you. Other than the hospital workers, you are all she has."

"Oh, Colleen, I promise to stay only long enough to pray. I feel laying hands on her, and praying is what she needs. She may not be responding to us, but she possibly can hear, that's why I feel so strongly about praying over her and aloud."

"Liz, if anyone here could reach her, I'm sure it would be you. God works through you, and everyone can feel it. You have been richly blessed in a very special way."

"Thank you, Colleen. I just do as I feel led."

Leaving the hospital, instead of going to work, Liz went back home. She knew the police had been their talking to Jana, Nina, and Gill. Maybe they had some information on the situation.

When Liz walked in, Jana came over to her. "How is the child doing? We have all been praying for her."

"Jana, she is in critical condition. The next twenty-four hours are critical as well. I know the police have been here. Do they have any idea who dropped her off at the door?"

"No, Liz, they questioned us, looked all around, and found nothing to go on. It's all such a mystery. Why would anyone want to beat someone like that?"

"I don't know, Jana, but I have got to find out. If she should survive, would they come back after her? I even wondered if maybe her parents were into drugs and were in some kind of trouble with a drug dealer, that things went bad, and the drug dealer took it out on that child. Maybe her mother has a boyfriend, and he was mad or upset and took it out on the girl. My mind has gone through so many scenarios. So many unanswered questions."

The side door opened, and Gill walked in. "The police have put yellow tape around the front where the girl was left. Blood is on the step, and they have a guy taking samples of the blood and anything else he can find. This is supposed to be a place to come to for safety, but with the police, the yellow tape and all, it could scare people off. Until they find out what really happened, I'm afraid no one will reach out to us for help."

"Oh, Gill, I hadn't thought of that. Do you think this will hurt us, Liz?" ask Jana.

"I don't think so, but I'm going to the police station and talk to them. I really don't want any information about this in the paper. Whoever dropped her off possibly thinks she is dead. If they find out she is still alive, they may come after her again. No, this needs to be kept quiet. Whoever dropped her off, if they can't find anything out in the paper, may come around to check on her. If they do, this could be a lead for us."

"Spoken like a true attorney," replied Jana. "Always turning every rock over for a clue or answer. I wonder if whoever dropped her here knew you were also a lawyer. Probably not and that's a good thing."

Patting Jana on the back, Liz said, "Okay, you guys go on about today as usual. Have any of our attendants been out front and questioned last night's happenings?"

"No, by it being in the evening, everyone was at the back of the house and was none the wiser. We haven't said a word, and the police didn't ask to question them. I think they were all watching television, which was a good thing," replied Gill.

"Well then, I am going to the police station and then to work. If you should need me, give me a call on my cell phone. I'm praying the rest of the day will be peaceful. After work, I plan to go by the hospital, so I'm not sure what time I'll be home."

Liz went out the back door but walked around to the front of the building. Sure enough, several strips of bright yellow tape were across the front area of the door. She hated to see this but hated more of what that poor girl had gone through before being placed there.

When Liz walked into the police station, Chief Craig Helton was standing there, as if waiting on her.

"Liz, I have been expecting you. You probably have lots of questions, but as of now, we have no answers."

"No, I'm not here with questions, but with a request. Please don't put any information about that girl in the paper. My reason is, whoever did this may possibly come around to see if she is still alive or dead. If they find out she is alive, they may come after her again. Not knowing the reason for the abuse, I need this case to be very tight-lipped."

Chief Helton said, "I will say, I must agree with you. This morning, as I went over everything at your place, something didn't seem quite right. I went up to the hospital and I could only see the girl through the window. I don't see how she can possibly make it. But whoever did this needs to pay. We need to know who is responsible for what has been done to her. If she lives, we can get some answers, but if she dies, we have so very little to go on."

Liz said, "Chief Helton, I believe she will live. Her recovery may be slow, for she has so much healing to do. At first, she may be reluctant to talk about it, but I believe she will come around in time. Right now, we must protect her from whoever did this. If they think she died and don't see an obituary in the paper, then they will start looking for her. We need to give her a name and pray it's not her real name."

Chief Helton rubbed his head. "Liz, I have no idea what to call the girl. She is so badly beaten. Do you have a name in mind?"

"Well, when I was in college, a girl in my class told me one day what her name meant in the Bible. Her name was Joanna and that means 'God is gracious.' I truly believe that God has a plan for her. Yes, she has suffered terribly, but look at Jesus, He suffered too. God graciously gave his Son for us, and I believe He has graciously given us this girl. Not to die, but to do good here on earth."

Taking a deep breath, Chief Helton shook his head. "Liz, if it was anyone else, I would probably not be so supportive, but you are an outstanding attorney. Since you have been here, you have taken on some tough cases and have not lost a one. Some I wasn't so sure about, but somehow you pulled it off. Okay, I'll give you some time and know, we are here backing you all the way."

"Oh, Chief Helton, thank-you, I promise you won't regret your decision."

"Liz, I have known your family for a long time. Good people and they raised an outstanding daughter. Millie, on the other hand, has made some very bad choices and I hate that for her and her parents. They are good people, too."

"We all make bad choices from time to time. Some choices seem a little more bitter than others, but still a bad choice is a bad choice. Some don't learn from those mistakes and keep making them. It takes them longer to see the wrong they are doing. They live in a fantasy world and not ready to grow up. If they would only learn to lean on God and trust him, have faith, and believe.

Like in Proverbs 3:5-6:

Trust in the Lord with all your heart and lean not on your own understanding; in all your ways acknowledge him, and he will make your paths straight.

Unfortunately, they don't want to listen and even turn away from God. It's sad, but I see it every day."

"I agree, for we see the same thing in here. You arrest a person, some go to jail for a while, and you would think when they got out, they would straighten up their lives. Some do, and a lot don't."

"Again, thank you, Chief Helton. I'll keep you posted on anything I find out."

"Liz, I'm going to get a device for you to wear just in case you encounter someone that could bring harm to you. It will be hidden under your clothes. We don't know who that girl is connected to, so for the time being, I want to know that you are alright."

"Do you really think that is necessary, Chief?"

"It's just for the time being. Better to be safe than sorry. Not that we are planning on anything bad happening, but I would feel safer if you wore it. I want you to even sleep with it on. The only time it is to be off is when you are taking a shower. I'm letting you do things your way for the time being, so let me do this for my peace of mind."

"Don't guess I'm in a position to say 'no'. Alright, so where do I go for my new accessory."

"Follow me, one of the female officers in the back will get you fitted up and show you how to take it off and put it back on."

Soon Liz was headed to her office. Knowing she was being tracked at her every move was a little unsettling. When she took the device off, she had to text them that she was taking a shower and then text that she was putting it back on. But she was in no position to disagree to do this, for Chief Helton was giving her time to do things her way. Hopefully, she wouldn't have to wear it for very long.

Liz had stayed late at work, trying to catch up on some paperwork since she was so late coming in. She also kept up with the time because she knew she needed to get to the hospital before the shift change, the new nurse coming on wouldn't be familiar with the girl's case. Grabbing her things, Liz headed out the door of her office. As she got off the elevator, and made her way to her car, she felt like someone was watching her. Although, she saw no one, reaching in her purse, she pulled out a taser. As she made her way to her car, she heard no noises, or saw any movement, but the feeling she was being watched stayed with her. As she got close to her car, her cell phone rang. Nearly jumping out of her skin, she looked down and it was Chief Helton calling.

"Hello, Chief."

"Hey, Liz. Is everything alright? The monitor you're wearing is showing your heart rate is up. What's that about?"

"I think it is just me. As I was walking to my car, I felt like I was being watched, but I don't see anyone. It's quiet here in the parking garage, just as always."

"It may be nothing, but I have already sent one of my men down to check. He should be coming through the stairway door any minute."

"Yes, I see him. It's Sergeant Drew Jordan."

"Good, he will make sure you leave the parking garage safely."

"Chief, you didn't tell me this monitor tracks my heart rate also!"

"Liz, that monitor you're wearing is for your safety. There very well could be someone watching you. I'm going to go over the camera from the garage and see if I see anything suspicious. In the meantime, don't take that monitor off. I'm going to have a patrol car be very close to wherever you are, so know, you are not totally alone. You go with your gut feelings and I'm going with mine right now."

"Chief, I appreciate all this, but I think you are being a little overprotective. Why would anyone want to hurt me?"

"Because that girl was left at your house and they may be watching to see where you're going, if it's to her or where. I'm sure they know she was taken away in an ambulance and needing to find out if she is dead or alive. You will be their source of information."

"I'm sure they want some information on her, that's why I don't want anything put in the paper. This needs to be kept very low key. I do appreciate your concern. I'm headed now for the hospital to check on her. Thanks again Chief."

Four

As Liz made her way down the hall at the hospital, she saw Colleen behind the nurse's desk. Liz lifted a prayer that the girl had made some improvement since she last saw her.

Looking up, Colleen said, "Hey, Liz, I was hoping you would come before I left. No changes at all. Occasionally you will hear a slight moan, but that's about it."

"I will take that as good news, for at least she hasn't taken a turn for the worst. I would like to go in and pray over her, but before I do, I want to discuss something with you. We know nothing about her, and it is possible that whoever did this maybe looking for her since nothing is in the paper. Chief Helton and I have decided to give her a name and no information or visitors are allowed."

"Liz, with her here in ICU, she is not permitted visitors anyway. You are only here because of me. Like I said earlier, I'm bending the rules for you to see her, but I feel you could be of help."

"Still, if she is connected to a gang or something, they might try to slip in. Anyway, the name we are giving her is Joanna. As of now, only you, Chief Helton and I know this name."

"Here on the floor, we refer to her as room two. It's also on her chart, room two."

"Good. I'm going to go on in and pray with her. For now, that's all I know to do."

Liz walked in and stood by the young girl. Nothing had changed since the last time she saw her. Her face was so badly swollen and discolored. Laying her hands so gently on the young girl, Liz began to pray.

When Liz came out, she had tears running down her cheeks. She told Colleen, "It breaks my heart to see her like this. I want so much to do something for her. I'm praying and know God is in control, but I want to do more."

Colleen walked over and put her arms around Liz. "I know what you're saying. I have gone in several times today and just stood by her and prayed. I truly believe that by hearing our voice, she knows we are trying to help her, and she is safe from harm. We are all she has for now and she maybe clinging to that. We have no idea what she is thinking or would want to say to us."

"I know. For some reason, that girl has touched my heart. I have dealt with many sad cases, but this one has engulfed me. I'll be back early in the morning. Will you be here?"

"Yes, I'm not off for three more days, but I'll make sure whoever is here will let you in to see her. Get some rest, Liz. If anything changes, I promise to let you know. Oh, by the way, Pastor Dotson came by today. He prayed outside her room and said he had called all the deacons together and they had prayer outside the hospital."

"Colleen, that is great. I will call Pastor Dotson and give him an update on her and let him know we need to keep this low key for her safety. See you in the morning."

When Liz went back to her car, she looked around and saw no one or anything that seemed different. As she pulled out of the parking lot, just around the corner sat Sergeant Jordan. As she passed him, he never acknowledged her, but she knew he would be close behind her very soon. Deep down inside, Liz felt at peace knowing she was being protected, but from what? That's the part that bothered her.

As she pulled in the garage at her home, her cell phone rang. It was Millie.

"Well, hello, how are things going for you?"

"Hey, Liz. Things are going well. I'm working at a hospital here in Raleigh. Glenda has helped me in so many ways. I can understand why you two were best friends in college. Her parents are wonderful as well. I feel like God has given me a second chance on life. No longer do I wake up in fear or worry of what may possibly go wrong with the day. All those guilt feelings I have been carrying around with me are going away, too."

"Millie, this is great news. Are you still living with Glenda, at the House of Blessings?"

"No, I moved out into an apartment not far from her or the hospital. I'm also going to church regularly at the church her father pastors. Liz, I know I have thanked you before for bringing me here, but you will never know how much this all has meant to me. You are the best cousin/sister anyone could want."

"Millie, if the situation was reversed, I'm sure you would have done the same for me. That's what family does, help each other out."

"I know, but when I look back at the day I brought Alex home for Thanksgiving, it wasn't just one person that had issues with him, it was the whole family, yet I turned blind eye. Instead of turning to God for advice, I tried to take matters into my own hands and blame others. Then I think of you in college, and how God put you and Glenda together as roommates. That was not just a coincidence, that was his plan. He knew what was in store for Glenda and that I would need her in the near future, also her House of Blessings would be waiting for me. Liz, I have so much to be thankful for. How are things with Aunt Dana and Uncle Ryan?"

"Can't complain. They are doing fine. How are things going with you and your parents?"

"We are all doing much better. In fact, I will be coming home in about two weeks. Dad and Mom have been so supportive, I just hate that I have put them through so much. I know Mom had so many plans for me and I really messed things up and hurt her deeply. By the way, have you found a guy yet? I'm sure in your line of work, you get a good range of available men."

"No, not really. I have gone out a few times with one guy, but with work and running my house I don't have very much free time."

"What was the name of your place again?"

"I called it, "Love by The Master.""

"Liz, where did you come up with that name?"

"Well, you know the house I was living in soon became too small. I went before the church and asked for prayer, that the home I had was longer big enough to take in the women that were in need. Do you remember shopping at Master's Department Store?"

"Oh, yes, I do. I loved shopping there. If I remember correctly, it had three floors, and every floor was fantastic."

"Well, Mr. and Mrs. Master came to see me one day at my office. They gave me the Master's building for my new home and even the things they sold at the closeout sale, they took that money and renovated the building so that it was feasible for me to take in women needing shelter. Since it was given in love by the Master family, I decided to call it 'Love by The Master.' Also, God, our heavenly Master, really coordinated it all ahead of time."

"Liz, this is wonderful. I wish I had kept my faith, did more praying and listening to God. But I let the devil in, and he took over. Nearly destroyed me, but I finally turned to God for help. I hope someday to come back home and when I do, I would like to help you in your home of love. I miss you, Liz."

"I miss you, too, Millie. Don't know if you heard, but Alex has remarried, and if rumor is correct, he will be moving to Ohio. His job is transferring him. Not sure of the date on that, but at least when you do come home, you won't have to worry about running into him."

"No, I hadn't heard that, but my heart goes out to whoever he has married. Hopefully, he has changed. He is one smooth talker, I'll say that about him. If I should ever decide to marry again, and my family shows signs of red flags, you can be sure I'll be paying attention."

Both girls laughed.

"Millie, I'm so glad you called tonight. Not only is it good to hear from you, but it's like old times again. I needed hearing from you, especially tonight. Been one of those days, if you know what I mean."

"Yes, I do. Thanks, Liz. I love you so much. You're the best."

"Love you, too, Millie."

When Liz walked in the door, Gill was standing there. "Any news on that poor girl?"

"I just left the hospital and no changes. By any chance has anyone come around asking questions other than the police?"

"No, it's been rather quiet. Apparently, none of the attendants saw or heard anything and no questions have been asked. I think they are all in their own little world, dealing with their own problems."

"That's good. Are Jana and Nina still here? I need to talk to all three of you about last night's events."

"Yes, come on in the kitchen. They have your dinner ready for you and we can all talk then."

Like Gill, Jana and Nina were eager to find out about the girl dropped off at the door, what her condition was, and if she was going to make it.

Liz explained what was going on and that they were not to give out any information. If anyone inquired, they were to tell them to contact the police.

Gill spoke up. "Liz, I went back and reviewed the footage on the camera we have outside our door. It showed someone with a black cap over them at the door and when they stepped back, the girl was there. It shows someone knocking at the door and then they left. I didn't realize the lights at the door were blown, so therefore it made it impossible to see very much. Lights from other buildings provided the only light we had."

"Gill, those lights should have been working. When we updated the cameras about two months ago, they replaced the bulbs. I wouldn't think they would have blown that quickly also that was good thinking about checking what was caught on film. With all that has happened, I had forgotten that. That reminds me of something else I need to talk to Chief Helton about, but that can wait till tomorrow. Gill, can you go back a few days and look to see if possibly someone had been tinkering with those lights?"

"Sure, Liz. Also, I have been thinking. You need someone here not only through the day, but at night."

"Gill, I'm here every night. If we have several ladies we are dealing with, one of you usually stays over. Besides, I have an alarm. If someone tries to break in, the alarm will go off."

"Gill's right," Nina spoke up. "From around nine at night till six the next morning, you are here by yourself. You really need to hire someone to work nights here or hire a security guard."

"Really, as busy as we have been, you should have a security guard around the clock," said Jana. "Or at least hire a man to always be on the premise. Gill is here a lot, but even through the day, he is sometimes out running errands and taking care of different things."

"Are you guys afraid when you are here?" Liz asked.

"Never have I ever given it a thought till Gill showed us the tape. When we are in here, we have no idea what's going on outside, especially at night," Jana replied.

"Let me think on this. I don't want to lose you guys and I want everyone safe. Anything else you need to share with me? When I'm at work, you guys are my eyes and ears. I depend on you so much."

"We love what we are doing," Jana said. "I think we can speak for Sandy, Myra, and Joe as well. This is our way of giving and helping. Anyone in the church will step up and help if one of us can't be here. What you are doing is a blessing and we all want to help and do our part."

"Jana is right," said Nina. "We can take this before the church and ask for help in security. We have some guys that are retired, and some that do work might consider doing a few weekends a month. Never hurts to ask."

Liz smiled. "I see you three have already been discussing this in depth."

"Not only that, but we contacted Sandy, Myra, and Joe to collect their thoughts. We are all in agreement," replied Nina.

"Being one of the deacons at our church, I don't feel we will have any problems with our request," said Gill. "If you give me the go ahead, I'll contact Pastor Dotson first thing in the morning."

"Well, I guess the matter is settled. I'll wait to hear what you find out and then at the next business meeting at church, we will bring this up."

"No, Liz. If the meeting with Pastor Rod Dotson goes well, we can have an urgent called business meeting after the service Sunday. No need dragging our heels for another month. I'll let you know as soon as I speak to him," Gill replied.

"Well, I guess things are settled for now, till we hear from Gill tomorrow. Now, I think I'll warm up my dinner."

Nina smiled. "It's already warm. While we were talking, I popped it in the microwave a second ago. Perfect timing."

While Liz ate, Gill went around and checked all the doors to make sure they were locked. As he, Jana, and Nina left, he set the alarm. As Liz sat their eating, she thought back over all that the three had said to her. She did not feel afraid and wondered if they knew something and weren't telling her. Ever since the events of that night, things had not been the same. Going back over every detail that she could remember since finding the girl at her door, she felt a clue was missing. She decided to ask to see the girls clothes the next morning, maybe something there might be a clue. Liz found a pen and paper and began making a list of things to look more deeply into.

Finally, deciding to call it a day, Liz cleaned up the dishes, then went upstairs for a shower. As she laid in bed, her mind would not stop working. Over and over, she kept replaying in her mind all that had taken place. The next thing she knew, her alarm was going off.

Liz said a prayer for the young girl before getting up.

"Dear Lord, we have this young girl who is seriously in pain. We know that no healing is too hard for You. Therefore, I pray that You bless her with Your loving care, renew her strength, and heal all that is broken and bruised in her body. In Jeremiah 30:17, it says, *'For I will restore health unto thee, and I will heal thee of thy wounds.' I believe this Father and I lift her up to you. Amen."*

Soon, Liz was on her way to the hospital. As she walked down the hall, she saw Colleen coming out of the girl's room.

"Morning, Liz, how are you?"

"Morning, Colleen. I'm doing well. How is our Joanna doing today? Did she have a good night?"

"I read what was documented on her when I came in and just checked all her vitals. Nothing has changed, which is good. She is holding her own. You can go on in. I have already had prayer with her, but I know you need your time, too. I need to check on another patient, so if I don't see you when you leave, I'll see you this evening."

Liz decided to call the girl the name they had given her. She leaned over and said, "Since we don't know your name, we are going to call you Joanna. It means 'God is gracious.' Then gently laying her hands on the young girl, Liz began to pray.

When she finished praying, she said, "I'll be back this evening to check on you. I want you to know, I am your friend. I love and care about you." Then she left to go to work.

Liz had just sat down at her desk when a knock came at her door. Chief Helton popped his head in. "Got a minute, Liz? I asked your secretary if you had anyone in here and she said, no."

"Sure, come on in, Chief. Just to let you know, I went by to check on our girl, and she is holding her own. This gives me hope that she is going to make it. She has a long road ahead of her, but I feel even more certain she will recover and then we can get some questions answered."

"That is good news. Liz, after you left last night, I went over the security camera footage, and nothing seemed out of the ordinary. I even checked to see who was assigned certain parking places and about the employees who park in there. Even had the guys to check who was a new hire that we may not know but came up with nothing. The last person hired was about three years ago, and he is a janitor who works days and occasionally works at night."

"I was going to ask you about that. Gill, one of the workers at my house, thought to check our camera footage. He saw someone with a dark cap over him and when he pulled back, the girl was on our steps. You could see a hand knock at the door, and then they left. For some reason, our lights outside our door were blown and the only light was from next door, making it very difficult to see anyone at the door."

"That's interesting, Liz. Did he go back on the footage to see if someone had been tinkering with the lights before all this?"

"Yes, and found nothing."

"Liz, I know you are not happy about the monitor you're wearing, but I feel it is very important that you keep it on. Something is amiss here and only time will tell."

"I will admit, I am not at all happy with this, but know, I will honor your wishes. Don't mean to cut this short, but I am due in court in a few minutes."

"No problem, Liz. Wanted to catch you before you got busy. Good luck in court today."

Gathering up her papers, Liz placed them in her briefcase. She had ten minutes to get to the courtroom and so thankful it was in the building today. Looking to see who the judge would be, Liz signed. Judge Noble Mize was all business. She liked him, but he was a stickler on facts.

He was one who wanted you to say what you had to say in twenty words or less. Most attorneys took that long to get started on what they wanted to say. But you learned quickly in Judge Mize's court to make it short and not necessarily sweet.

Five

Two weeks passed and Joanna was still in critical condition. The staff at the hospital worked continually with her, and Liz stopped by twice a day to pray. The blood samples taken from the steps of Liz's home proved to be Joanna's blood. A strand of hair was found on the steps, but that too, was Joanna's. After visiting and having prayer, Liz stopped outside the hospital and considered what little they had learned. She had to be overlooking something. A guy about Liz's age stopped and said, "Excuse me, but are you Liz Barnett, an attorney?"

Liz said, "Why are you asking?"

The guy smiled and said, "A good friend of mine a few years ago needed an attorney. I believe that was you. He was wrongfully accused of doing something he didn't do, and you were wonderful. I wanted to thank-you and let you know should I ever need an attorney; you are the one for me."

"What was your friend's name?" she asked.

"Edgar Sloan."

"Yes, I remember him, and you were always there, so positive and supporting him. Scott, I think, is your first name?"

"You have a great memory. My last name is Hunter. Scott Hunter."

"What is Mr. Sloan doing now?"

"We both live in Raleigh, North Carolina, and both are doctors. I'm here visiting a good friend from school."

"Congratulations on becoming a doctor, and I hope your friend here is a doctor as well and not a patient."

"No, he's not a doctor, he's a patient. He has some health issues and he asked for me to come visit him. He wants advice on what he should do."

"I wish him well and so glad you stopped and introduced yourself to me. Tell Mr. Sloan I said 'Hello' and I wish both you gentlemen the best in your career."

As they parted ways, Liz happened to think about Millie. Turning to see if Scott Hunter was close by, she called out, "Dr. Hunter."

He turned to see what Liz needed.

"Yes."

"My cousin works at Duke University. She is a physician assistant. By any chance, do you work at Duke?"

"Yes, I do. What is your cousins name?"

"Millie Barnett. She just recently became a physician assistant."

"No, the name doesn't ring a bell, but if our paths happen to cross, I'll introduce myself to her."

"I know Duke is a big hospital, thought I would ask. You have a blessed day." Liz turned to go find her car and head home.

When Liz walked in the door, Nina came rushing up to her.

"Liz, a man came by looking for his daughter today. He has only been gone about fifteen minutes. He said she had run away from home, and he was hoping maybe she had come here. He said her name was Carrie. I told him we didn't have a Carrie and that he should report this to the police. He asked if he could look around and I told him no visitors were allowed. He seemed upset with me and wanted to speak to the owner. I told him to check back around six. My first thought was could he be the one who put our Joanna at the doorstep."

Surprised, Liz said, "This is interesting. Finally, someone has come looking for a young girl."

Liz looked at her watch. It was five thirty-five. This gave her some time to collect her thoughts and be prepared for whoever the man was.

At six o'clock, a man opened the door and walked up to the desk, where Liz was sitting.

"Excuse me, but I am looking for the owner of this place. Is it possible I can speak to him?"

Liz stood up. "I'm the owner, how can I help you?"

The man looked surprised to find out a woman was the owner. "I'm sorry, I was expecting a man, not a woman."

"No problem. How can I help you?"

Clearing his throat, he said, "You see I have a teenage daughter that her mother and I have a very hard time dealing with. She is very rebellious. From time to time, she runs away from home and this time, I haven't been able to find her. I have looked at places she would normally hide, but this time I have had no luck. Her mother is worried sick. As a last resort, I was hoping I could find her here. Her name is Carrie."

"I'm sorry sir, but we don't have any one by that name."

"Is it possible that I can look around. She may have given you a different name."

"Sir, this is a safe home. We don't allow visitors here. Can you give me a description of her? What color hair, eyes, weight, and how tall she is?"

"Carrie may have dyed her hair since we last saw her. Like I said, she is a troubled child and likes to cause trouble."

"Again, if you can give me a description of her, I will know if she is here? Have you been to the police?" Liz asked.

"No. You don't seem to understand. Carrie has run away several times, she lies and can't be trusted. If we call the police every time she runs away, we are afraid she will be sent off to a home for unruly children. She doesn't realize how much she is breaking her mother's heart. She is our only child, and you could say we spoiled her when she was little and now we are paying for it. We just want our daughter home with us. "

"I understand, Sir, but we have rules here and we cannot bend them for anyone. Leave me your name and number, should she come by, I will give you a call."

"Why don't I stop by in a few days and check to see if she is here? Should she come by, with the way she lies, I ask that you don't call the police. I'm sure her story would be much different from mine. You would think her mother and I are terrible parents, but the truth of the matter is, we simply love her so much."

Liz looked at the man, studying him closely. "Sir, you still haven't given me a description of your daughter. We have several people come through our door in need of help. Without a description, how will I know if it's your daughter?"

"You will know her. She is very fidgety. Always moving, never standing still. She has a problem of looking straight at you, as if she is hiding something."

"Also, do you remember what she was wearing the last time you saw her?" Liz asked.

"No, I don't. She took some of her clothes with her, so I have no idea what she is wearing."

"Does she have any body piercings or tattoos?

"No, she would never do that. Like I said, she is different from your other teenagers. She just can't be trusted, that's why it is so important to find her. I'll check back in in a few days to see if she has come by."

With that the man turned and walked out the door. Liz had the same feeling come over her that she had when she first met Alex Sailor. Deep down, she knew the man was lying and wondered if Joanna was who he was looking for. All he had given her was the name Carrie. No description of any kind.

Nina walked over to where Liz was. "For whatever good it may do, I took a picture of that man on my cell phone just in case we need it for later. I know we have cameras here, but I wanted to make sure we got a close shot of him. Took a few as he turned his head."

"Nina, he didn't see you, did he?" Liz asked.

"No, he was too busy trying to convince you he was looking for his problem child. That man gives me the creeps. Something about him just isn't right and I think you will agree."

Just then the front door opened and Millie walked in.

"Hey, Liz." Walking over to give her cousin a big hug, "How are things going?" Millie asked.

"Oh, Millie, it's so good to see you, and you look absolutely wonderful. You are a ray of sunshine."

"I guess so, after what just left your building. I ran into some creepy guy coming out your door. He nearly knocked me down. Never said a word to me, but the look on his face. Let's just say he was not a very happy person. Actually, a bad feeling came over me. What was he doing here?"

"Trying to get some information from us. As you know, we are not permitted to discuss anyone that comes in here for protection or whatever they need."

"Well, if you ask me, that guy needs some help, some serious help. Hope he doesn't come back here. Are you not afraid, Liz, of people like him coming in here?"

"No, not really. You see Millie, we have security cameras everywhere and we also have a security guard here."

"Liz, how are you making it financially? I know you make good money, but how are you affording all of this?"

"Millie, we rely on God. As I have told you, the Master's gave us the building and they send the church a check every few weeks that goes into a fund for this place, plus several from the church drop a check into the offering plate for here. This is how we purchase food, pay the utilities and things like that. We have people from the church that volunteer to work. Security guards are retirees from the church, and some that are still working may come in every few months to do volunteer work on the weekend or their day off. God has worked it out so beautifully. We even have a pantry that brings food by. Our shelves are never bare."

"Liz, I do wish I had your faith. Growing up, you were always the strong one in your walk with God. Me, I would follow along with you, but my heart wasn't where yours was. Look at us, you still listen to God; me, I always listened to others that made things sound good."

"Don't be so hard on yourself, Millie. We all make mistakes, but look at you. You learned from the school of hard knocks and now doing so much better. I am really proud of you, and I know Uncle Roy and Aunt Debbie are, too."

"Thanks, Liz, I wish I could redo that part of my life, but I can't. I hope to help others that may be heading in that direction. I can give them firsthand advice and hope they listen and not be like I was."

"So, what are your plans for dinner tonight?" Liz asked.

"I called Mom and told her I was coming in, and she is fixing dinner for me. Knowing her, she has cooked enough for an army. Say, why don't you come and have dinner with us tonight? I'm sure they wouldn't mind."

"Oh, Millie, I know they wouldn't mind, but I see them more often than you do. You need to spend this time with them. How long are you going to be home?"

"Almost a week. But I plan to come back in for the Fourth of July, at least that's my goal."

"Before you go back, we will have to spend a day together, go out have some fun. I'm sure between the two of us, we can find something to get into!" Liz said.

Both girls laughed then hugged each other.

Smiling, Liz had a tear to come to her eyes. "Millie, this is like old times. It's so good to have you home and I look so forward to our day together."

"I know exactly what you mean. I love you, Liz. You're the best cousin/sister anyone could have."

Millie left to go visit her parents. As soon as she was gone, Nina came back into the room.

"I looked at the pictures I took of that guy, and I got some good close-up shots. When your cousin came in, I wanted to give you some time with her, and it gave me a chance to look at the pictures. Liz, I have never seen him around here anywhere and something about him is not right. I wonder if he has a wife and if that poor girl that was dropped off is the one he is looking for."

"My thoughts exactly, Nina. I wonder if he was trying to find out if she was alive or dead. If you don't mind, make a copy of those pictures and when the time is right, I'll show them to Chief Helton. For now, I'm going to wait and see if he comes back around."

When the weekend came, Liz and Millie decided to spend the day together. They went shopping, ate, and shopped some more. Later in the day, they decided to go for a walk in the park. The day was absolutely gorgeous. Very few clouds in the sky, a slight breeze blowing, perfect for taking a walk. As they were walking, Liz had the same strange feeling as before that she was being watched. She looked around and didn't see anything out of the ordinary. Millie was chatting away, but Liz couldn't shake the feeling. Soon her phone rang, it was Chief Helton.

"Liz, Chief Helton here. Is everything alright?"

"Yes, I'm at the park enjoying some time with my cousin. Anything going on?"

"Well, you tell me. Your monitor shows you're a little anxious about something, so what's going on?"

"Honestly, Chief, my cousin and I are taking a nice walk in the park today. It is so nice outside. You should get away from your office and enjoy this beautiful day."

"Liz, I'm at home, sitting outside enjoying the day. Your monitor is attached not only to the office but to my phone. I told you; I was going to keep track of you. I feel you could possibly be in danger of some kind, and we are going to stay on top of it. Sorry to have bothered you but until some things are settled, you may be getting a call from me time to time. I know you don't like it, but when the monitor goes off, I need to hear from you, it gives me peace of mind. Enjoy the rest of your day with your cousin."

Then he hung up.

Millie looked at Liz. "Who was that?"

"It has to do with work. I'm not really in any position to talk about it. Now, what were we talking about before I received that phone call?"

Deep down inside, Liz hated wearing that monitor and it bothered her more that every time her heart raced a little, Chief Helton or someone from the police station was calling her. She had thought about not wearing it, but she had promised Chief Helton she would. She did not want to go back on her word, and in all reality, it may be a good thing till they could at least find out something from Joanna. The poor girl was healing, but she was still in a coma. So many questions and it all hinged on Joanna waking up and being able to talk. Liz prayed every day the girl would wake up and be willing to talk and could provide information about her attacker.

"Liz, are you listening to me? Where is your mind?" Millie asked.

"Millie, I'm so sorry. A lot is going on at work and I promised myself this morning that I would leave work alone today. I'll save those thoughts for Monday. Today, it's about us. Now, what were you saying?"

Six

onday morning came way to early. Liz had spent Saturday with Millie and Sunday with the rest of the family. It brought back so many memories. How she needed this time and them. In fact, they all needed this time together. Millie had promised to come home for the Fourth of July and so they all started making plans.

When Liz pulled up at the hospital to go visit Joanna, the feeling she was being watched came over her again. Trying hard to keep her heart at a normal rate so the monitor would not show anything, she decided to go through the emergency room door. Maybe if she was being watched, it would throw someone off. Once inside, she took the stairs to the floor where Joanna was. Not thinking, the four flights of stairs would get her heart rate up. Soon her phone was ringing.

"Ms. Barnett, this is Sergeant Drew Jordan. Is everything okay with you?"

"Yes, Sergeant Jordan. I have been walking up four flights of stairs and it sort of winded me. Forgot about my monitor. I do apologize."

"No problem, Ms. Barnett, as long as you're alright. May I ask you a question? Why did you use the stairs? Is there a problem with the elevator?"

"Just trying to get in a little exercise. I'm at a desk all day and thought the steps would be a good way to start my day. Thank you for checking on me."

Liz hung up the phone and thought trying to avoid being followed was impossible. As she walked down the hall to Joanna's room, she prayed today would be the day that Joanna would wake up. When she got to Joanna's room, Liz froze in her tracks, the room was empty. Turning to the nurse's station, Liz looked around for a nurse. Finally, she spotted one in a small room over to her left in a corner.

"Excuse me," Liz asked. "Do you know where the patient is that was in room 2-B?"

The nurse looked at Liz, recognizing her from her visits, replied, "Let me call Nurse Rivers, she can answer your questions."

The nurse went around the corner into a small room and closed the door. Liz had a thousand things going through her mind about Joanna. Why hadn't Colleen called her if something had come up? Maybe the girl coded, and they didn't have time to call. Maybe they had to rush her into surgery or hopefully she had improved and was moved to another room, but then Colleen would have called her.

The nurse came out of the small room and said, "Nurse Rivers will be here to talk to you in a few minutes. You are welcome to have a seat here, while you wait for her."

"Thank you, but I'll stand," was all Liz could say.

While waiting, Liz walked to the lobby area near the elevators. She walked over to the big double windows and looked out. As she looked below at the people coming and going, she noticed near a tree was a man looking up at the hospital. He had on the same clothes that the man was wearing that came to her house asking about his daughter. She tried so hard to make out his facial features but with his hat, it was impossible. Could this possibly be the same man and was he following her, was that why she kept having those feelings of being watched?

"Liz!"

Colleen had walked up behind her and being so deep in thought Liz didn't hear her. She jumped like she had been shot.

"Colleen, what's going on? Why is Joanna not in her room?"

"Liz, I'm sorry, I didn't mean to scare you. Come with me and we will talk somewhere more private."

Liz's phone rang again. It was Sergeant Jordan.

"Ms. Barnett, anything going on at the hospital that you're not telling me?"

"No, I'm so sorry. I was waiting on a nurse to come out to talk to me and I was deep in thought and didn't hear her walk up. Forgot about the monitor."

"No problem. Hate to keep calling you, but we have to make sure you are alright."

"Thanks, Sergeant Jordan. I'll try to do better, at least for the rest of the day."

"No worries. Stay safe."

Turning to Colleen, Liz said, "Sorry, now about Joanna!"

"Come with me," and Colleen went down a hall.

Following Colleen, Liz was filled with more suspicion on what was going on. Trying to brace herself for the possibility that something was wrong with Joanna, she prayed as they walked to a different area of the hospital.

"Here, let's talk in here." Colleen said.

As they walked into the room, Liz looked around and it was basically a room with only three chairs and a small table over on one side. Very sterile.

"Have a seat and we will talk. I came in here for a reason and I think you will understand after we talk."

Taking a seat, Liz still looked around and studied the room very carefully. Why only three chairs and a small table and why this room to talk in? Something was not right.

"Liz, I know you have lots of questions and I will answer them after I explain some things. Let me start by saying Joanna is alright. She is in a safe place, but we felt it best to move her. Last night around nine o'clock a man came on the floor looking for a young lady that may possibly be her. We are not sure how he got through the doors that enter the ICU unit unless he slipped in when one of us opened the door to go either in or out. Again, we are not sure. Anyway, one of the nurses spotted him coming down the hall. She immediately went to him and explained he couldn't be here on this floor. He told her his daughter had been in an accident and he was told she was here in the ICU unit. She asked him who sent him here and he said the captain of the police department. She explained that still he would have to wait out in the visitors lounge and ask for his daughter's name. He told her, Carrie, that she changed her last name often and he didn't have any idea, what last name she went by at the present."

Liz turned pale. "Did he say if she was a young girl. In her teens?"

"All she was able to get from him was that his daughter was a young girl, and her name was Carrie. He didn't want to leave, He wanted to look around to see if his daughter for sure was here."

"The man that came to the house looking for his daughter said her name was Carrie." replied Liz.

"This is possibly the same man, but Nurse Martin said something about the man made her very uneasy. Another nurse had walked up to the nurse's station and Nurse Martin turned to her and said we have a code gray on the floor. This let her know help was needed here quickly. The man tried to walk around Nurse Martin and just as she stepped in front of him, Chief Helton walked in. He was unaware of the situation and did not realize they had sent out a call for code gray."

"What was Chief Helton doing here last night?" ask Liz.

"Call it a blessing from God, for you know how God works. Anyway, when Chief Helton walked in, the man turned to leave. Nurse Martin quickly explained to the chief about the man looking for his daughter that had been in an accident. Chief Helton went back outside to where the man was waiting at the elevator. They talked, then the man left, and Chief Helton came back in. I was called to come into work, for the Chief wanted to talk to me. It has been a long night, but Chief Helton and I both agree, the man is looking for our Joanna. We have moved her to a place that she should be safe and will have an officer outside her door."

"Why not leave here where she was and put an officer outside that door?" asked Liz.

"Where we have her, she is the only patient. Here, we do have family members coming in at certain times and can only stay so long. We didn't want an officer outside her door or any door with other families coming and going, trying to keep down any talk. Besides, if you are being followed, which the Chief thinks you are and won't admit it, it will be harder for him to get to her where she is."

"Why does the Chief think I'm being followed?" Liz asked with curiosity.

"That I don't know. He wouldn't go into much detail. He asked a lot of questions and wants answers, but if you ask him something, he is very vague. I told him two could play his game. In fact, a little later in our conversation, he asked me about some things regarding Joanna's condition. I stated she was improving. When he started asking questions about certain things, my replied was, 'she is improving.' I think he got my message."

"Colleen, I feel the need to see Joanna every day and pray over her."

"Liz, I understand. For I read to her from the Bible daily and pray over her, but you might want to consider staying away for a few days just in case this guy is following you and trying to find out about his daughter."

"I wonder if she is his daughter, or if he has kidnapped her. A lot to think about, for this man isn't your average guy. Also, if she was kidnapped, why would he beat her unless he was holding her for money, and someone is refusing to pay? The questions can go on and on."

"Liz, you said a minute ago, a man had come to your house looking for a young girl and he said her name was Carrie! What did that man look like?"

"I guess he was about forty, maybe in his thirties. Average build. Had on dark blue pants, dark stripped shirt, black jacket, and a black hat with a big brim."

"That's the same description Nurse Martin gave me. She also said his eyes looked like they were looking through you. He gave her the creeps."

"Yes, I remember those eyes. You don't forget them easily."

"Chief Helton was going to have someone from his office to do a sketch of the man to have on file. He thinks this man is looking for Joanna and possibly try to finish her off. That's why she has been moved."

"Colleen, you mentioned Chief Helton came to Nurse Martin's aid when they had given out a code gray. How did he get through those doors? Does he have a code he uses that let himself in, like what I use?"

"No, there had been a bad wreck earlier and one of the victims was admitted to the ICU unit. He was here following up on that wreck and one of the nurses had let him in. He was on his way out when this all happened. That's why I said, God was working things out at the exact right time."

"I will say, in all my time working here in Nashville, I have never dealt with a case like this. When I get back to work, I'll check through some records to see if this man may have a criminal history. So, may I go back and see Joanna?" Liz asked.

"Yes, but remember, you must curtail your visits. It's for Joanna's sake and I promise to keep you posted every day about her. One other thing, Liz. You need to be more aware of your surroundings. This guy may be looking at you as his next victim. Never know what's going through people's minds these days."

"Colleen, I'm an attorney, that's one thing they caution you about in school and for good reason. I do appreciate your concern for me, you are truly a wonderful friend."

"I just don't want you to end up here as one of my patients. If you will follow me, we'll go see Joanna."

Colleen took Liz down a hall, through some double doors and down another hall. Finally, they came to Joanna's room. Over on the other side of the hall sitting at a table was a police officer but dressed in scrubs. Liz had to sign a book he had before entering Joanna's room. Even Colleen signed the book. Everything was being documented. They even ran a detector over her, and her purse was checked. Liz carried a gun and had to leave it at the desk with the police officer. Once inside, Liz noted that Joanna was still the same. No improvement. The child had gone through so many surgeries and tests, still in a coma. All her bruises were gone, and her broken bones had healed. If she could only wake up and talk to them, so many questions could be answered on a table beside Joanna's bed was a Bible and that's all Liz needed.

Leaning over Joanna, Liz spoke to her. "This is Liz, your friend. I'm here to help you and read to you this morning."

Opening the Bible, Liz read some scripture from I Corinthians 13:4-8.

Love is patient, love is kind. It does not envy, it does not boast, it is not proud. It does not dishonor others, it is not self-

seeking, it is not easily angered, it keeps no record of wrongs. Love does not delight in evil but rejoices with the truth. It always protects, always trusts, always hopes, always perseveres. Love never fails.

With that, Liz stop reading and placed her hand over Joanna's. "Someday, my child, you will understand about love, especially the love that God gives."

After praying, Liz left to go back to work but left through another entrance, even though it meant a longer walk to her car. Still if she was being watched, it would hopefully throw the person off.

Arriving at her office, Liz was met in the hall by Chief Helton.

"Liz, if you have a moment, I would like to talk to you. I know you probably have a busy schedule today, but I feel this is important and you can possibly fill in some blanks for me."

"Sure, Chief, come on in."

Upon entering her office, Liz stopped by the receptionist desk. "Dee, I need to talk to Chief Helton for a few minutes. What does my schedule look like for the next twenty to thirty minutes?"

"Miss Barnett, you are clear for that amount of time. I will hold all your calls also."

"Thank- you, Dee."

Turning to Chief Helton, "Would you care for a cup of coffee?"

"No, I have already had way more than I need, but thanks anyway."

Closing the door behind her, Liz walked over and sat down behind her desk. She motioned for Chief Helton to have a seat.

"So, tell me, what's on your mind? I'm still wearing the monitor, so you know everywhere I go. Is it possible I can take this monitor off for good?"

"No, Liz, that monitor is yours for a while yet. Sorry, I know that is not what you want to hear. What I want to talk to you about, I was at the hospital on a call early this morning. There was a bad wreck in town, and I was following up on it. I happened to walk in as a nurse gave out a code gray. I was unaware that she had given out that code and the man in front of her turned and left to go to the elevators. She shared briefly about the man, so I went to the elevator to speak to him. After we spoke, I went back in to talk to Nurse Martin. She contacted Nurse Rivers. After speaking in dept to Nurse Rivers, we both agreed the man was looking for Joanna. We had the young girl moved to a more secure area and in the meantime, I had my guys come over and do a fingerprint check. They were able to lift several prints, plus his whole left hand. At the moment, this is being checked out. As you know, once the fingerprints are analyzed using our computerized system it will search various local, state, and national fingerprint databases for a match. This could possibly take some time. Also, I had one of the guys do a sketch of him this morning for me. This could help in our search through the records. Meantime, I am concerned for your safety. This man would not state his name, the only name he revealed was his daughter, name. Carrie."

Leaning back in her seat, Liz asked. "Do you think this man has a record and is possibly dangerous?"

"Don't you think so, Liz? Why else would your heart monitor go off as often as it does? When you are here at work, it's fine. When you are home, it's fine. When you are at the hospital or near it, or in your car, your heart rate jumps up. Why did you take the steps at the hospital this morning? Who were you trying to avoid? Yes, my men report to me any activity your monitor shows. I will have to say, you did some quick thinking when Sergeant Jordan contacted you. Taking the stairs for exercise. Good reply, Liz."

"The man in question, do you think he will go back to the hospital and try to locate Joanna? What if he does find her and she is not his daughter? We could be protecting her from the wrong person."

"Nice try, Liz. Let's go back to my questions that you seem to be avoiding and then we will address your questions. Now, when you are out, do you feel as if this man is watching or following you?"

"Sometimes I do get the feeling I am being watched, but I'm an attorney, any of my clients could spot me when I'm out."

"Liz, stop. You know exactly what I am getting at. You attorneys have a way of turning things around for your own good. Now shoot straight with me. I am here to help and protect you. If I can find anything about this guy, I'm bringing him in. I feel you know more than you are willing to share with me. This guy could be dangerous, and if he is trying to get to that girl, he may not think twice about taking you out to get to her."

"I understand everything you are saying, and I would like nothing more than to find out who this man is and who that young girl in the hospital really is. If she could wake up, she could fill in a lot of blanks that we have. My greatest fear is that when she does wake up, what she has gone through was so traumatic that it will all be blocked from her mind. That has happened to people before. I am willing to go to whatever lengths I need to go in order to protect her. In fact, I have a wonderful friend in North Carolina that I have seriously thought about sending Joanna to. She is the one that help me start my home for women here. They have a wonderful hospital where Joanna could go for any help or treatment she may need. I'm just not sure about sending her until she wakes up. And for the record, you also have a way of avoiding certain issues that you don't want to discuss. So don't go picking on attorneys."

"You know Liz, that is not a bad idea. Then we could focus on two people instead of three."

"Chief Helton, if Joanna is in North Carolina, our focus would be on only one person."

"No Liz, we still have you to watch out for. We have no idea what is going through that man's mind, and even if Joanna goes to North Carolina, you still have to wear that monitor. I want to know more about him. I had one of my men go over to your place and make a copy of the tape of the day the guy showed up at your place when he was inquiring about his daughter. I also want a copy of the picture you have of him. We are going to work on this case together. Until I get the answers I want, my department is going to become your new best friend or sidekick."

"What picture are you talking about?"

"One of your workers took his picture the day he stopped by your place. Remember that? Well, when one of my men was going over some things, let's say at the crime scene, they made the comment it would help if they could get a good picture of him. Jana informed him that Nina had a picture of him on her phone."

Standing up to leave, Chief Helton looked at Liz, "Sending that girl to North Carolina is a great idea. See if you can make that happen."

Turning, he walked out the door.

Deep down inside, Liz knew Chief Helton was right. Sending Joanna to North Carolina would be a good move, and she felt like the man was not only after the girl but her as well. But what if Joanna was not Carrie? Could they be suspecting the wrong person? The man did not want to reveal much information and Joanna was in no condition to help them on the facts. So many unanswered questions, but at this point, they could not take any chances. She texted Colleen to call her when she had some time. She needed to find out if Joanna could be moved, then she would call Glenda and see what she could do on her end. In the meantime, they would have to keep up their guard.

Seven

ate that night, Colleen called Liz.

"Liz, sorry I am so late getting back with you, but it has been a busy day. Eating today was take a bite of food and keep going. I'm sure you have had those days. So, what's up?"

"Colleen, if you want to go home and relax, we can talk tomorrow. It's nothing that can't wait."

"No, I'm sitting in traffic and it's not moving, so talking to you will help pass the time."

"Bless your heart. After a long day at work, you don't need this, but that's the way things usually go."

"I know, but this is life, so, what would you like to talk about?"

"How is our Joanna doing?" Liz asked.

"About the same. Sometimes she will moan but that's all. I still go in and pray with her. If time permits, I read the Bible to her and always let her know she is safe, and we are there for her. There is a monitor in her room where we can watch any movement she may make, but so far nothing."

"Colleen, do you think she could be moved to another facility? Say, out of state? Chief Helton and I have been talking. We know she has been moved to a safer place at the hospital but if she was in another state where we are not being watched, and if she did wake up and need therapy or whatever, they could work with her without fear of this man making his way into the hospital."

"Liz, she is in a safe area. We even have a security guard outside her door. No one can get inside to her."

"But what if she wakes up? She has not stood and walked in a long time. She is going to need therapy for that, and I'm sure for the abuse she has been through, she will need counseling. If she was in another state, what would the chances be of that man finding her? If we are not visiting her, he may think she has passed away. We feel she would be much safer and away from any threat that she may have here."

"I don't know. I'll have to talk to Dr. Lucas. He is her attending doctor here at the hospital, and she can't be moved without his approval. There is a lot to be considered. First of all, she is a minor and has no family that we are aware of. Second, she is still in a coma."

"Are you working tomorrow Colleen or is that your day off?"

"No, Liz, I'm working. I can send him a text saying that a meeting is needed regarding Joanna and that you and Chief Helton want to be present. I'll let you know what his reply is and all I can say is that you need to come prepared to present your case well. Everyone has become very attached and protective of Joanna on the floor."

"I know, Colleen, I feel the same way, but if we could somehow get this man off her trail, she would be so much better off."

"Liz, what if the man that says he is looking for his daughter Carrie, really is and his story is true. We could be protecting her from the wrong person."

"All the more reason to send her to another state. We have too many missing pieces, and we need to protect her every way we can."

"Like I said, I'll send Dr. Lucas a text and get back with you when I hear from him. In the meantime, I'm going to do some praying. Not sure of my feelings on all this and certainly not what I was expecting when I returned your call tonight."

"Thanks, Colleen. What we are doing is for her best interest, that's what we must stay focused on, until she wakes up and can speak for herself."

Hanging up the phone, Liz began to pray. She had to pray and ask for guidance on what was best for Joanna. Selfishly, she wanted to keep the girl here and be able to visit her every day, to watch for progress and to be by her side should she wake up. But this wasn't about her, it was about a young girl that needed the right kind of protection.

The next morning Liz put a call in to Glenda. If she could get Joanna in a hospital in Raleigh, she knew the girl would be in good hands. She needed to have answers should Colleen arrange an appointment for her and Chief Helton to speak to Dr. Lucas. Liz knew Glenda would be there for Joanna as well as Millie if they could get her transferred. Again, so many "ifs." Closing her eyes, Liz lifted a prayer for God's hand to be present in all that were involved in this case.

The next morning at work, Liz's personal phone rang. It was Nina.

"Hey, Nina, is everything alright at the house?"

"Liz, that man came by again asking if by any chance his daughter was here. I told him no and that he really should report this to the police. Gill happen to walk in and tried to talk to the man. All we could get from him was the same story as before, that he was looking for his daughter and her name was Carrie. Gill offered to pray with him and tried to get a description of the girl. The man wanted to look around and stated he felt we were hiding her and that his wife was beside herself with worry. He did say his wife was not well and it was important that he find Carrie."

"Nina, I don't understand why he doesn't want to talk to the police or file a missing person report. By any chance did he ask to speak to me?"

"No, he didn't mention you at all. He had on the same clothes as before. Do you think he is looking for our Joanna or do you think he has a daughter that is a run-away?"

"Nina, I just don't know. It doesn't make sense to me. Deep down, I feel he is looking for Joanna and he is the one who dropped her off at our door. Since I have stopped going by the hospital as often, he may think she is well and living with us."

"Or he may wonder if she has passed away and we will offer some information. Liz, this guy still gives me the creeps. I was so thankful when Gill walked in, he had no idea the man was in the room. God was definitely watching over us as He always does. I couldn't help but say 'Thank You, Lord'."

"Thanks, Nina, for letting me know. This information is very important. Make sure a man is always around when you ladies are working. Hopefully that man won't come back, but in case he does, I don't want you ladies to be there without some support."

"Don't worry, Liz. Joe, the security guard from church, had just left when Gill came in. He had told Gill some men from other churches wanted to volunteer to help and they were working on a new schedule. That man may give me the creeps, but God has his army protecting us. Everyone here is alright, I thought you might want to know what had taken place here this morning."

"Keep me posted should anything new happen."

Liz took out a folder that had her notes regarding Joanna. She looked over them, searching for some clue. What was she missing? Closing the folder, she bowed her head and ask God to open her eyes, show her what she needed to see. Months had gone by and still nothing but questions. Never had she came across anything so difficult.

Liz's phone buzzed; it was her secretary Dee, letting her know she was due in court in an hour, and the information she had asked for was ready. The case she had coming up was easy, for which Liz was grateful. Judge Mize was presiding over the case, so things should go smoothly.

By the time Liz got back to her office, she had messages that Glenda, Chief Helton, and Colleen had called. Looking at the list, she decided to call Glenda first. Dialing the number, it went straight to her voice mail, just her luck. She had to leave Glenda a message, so Liz decided to grab a bite to eat. She really wanted to talk to Glenda first, then depending on her answers, she would know what to do next.

On her way back to the office, her phone rang. Without looking to see who was calling, Liz said, "Hello."

"Liz, are you busy? Have I called at a bad time?"

"No, Millie, what's up?"

"Well, I'll be coming home next weekend and wanted to make sure you would be free."

"I should be, can't think of anything right off that I have planned. I didn't think you were coming home till around July! You're not bringing home a guy, are you?"

"Now, Liz, do you think I would do that?"

"Well, you seem very chipper and happy, so I can't help but wonder if a man is in the picture."

Laughing, Millie said, "You are just going to have to wait till next weekend and find out. I called ahead so you could have someone cover your weekend at the house for you. I know you always try to stay there on the weekends and give the other workers the weekend off."

"You are not going to believe this, but we have so many volunteers that want to work one day a week, which is wonderful. This way no one gets burned out and if someone needs time off, we have the coverage. God has really blessed our shelter and the workers are all so godly and want to help these ladies in need.

"Liz, I understand exactly what you are saying. Glenda has so many helpers and they have such a heart in helping. It is amazing. I go over and help some on my days off, and those ladies simply soak up the love you pour out to them. I can relate and it makes giving and loving on them so easy for me. It holds a very special place in my heart and always will. Now, about next weekend. Can you be free Saturday through Monday?"

"I'm not at the office at the moment, so I can't say about Monday. What exactly do you have planned?"

"Just text me about Monday when you find out. I'm so excited about coming home. See you then, Liz. Love you."

Millie hung up before Liz had a chance to say anything else. Liz wondered what Millie was planning and what she needed three days for, when her thoughts were interrupted by her phone ringing. It was Glenda.

"Glenda, hey, girl, how are you?"

"Hey, Liz. Doing great. So how can I help you? I listened to your message and hope I can be of assistance."

"This is about the young girl I have spoken to you about before. She is still in a coma and has been moved to a more private area of the hospital. Not knowing if the person who is responsible for putting her in this condition is still looking for her, we were wondering if she is approved to be transported would it be possible to transport her to a hospital near you, and if they would accept her. I'm waiting on a meeting now to speak to the hospital here about moving her, but I need to be able to tell them where she can be taken. We have given her a first name, but still don't know anything else."

"Liz, I personally know several doctors at a hospital here. We have worked on other cases, and I don't think there should be a problem. I will text you the name and phone number of a doctor that can really be very beneficial. Duke University has some excellent doctors that can help her when she does wake up."

"Oh Glenda, this is wonderful. This girl means so much to me and I want only the very best for her."

"I will let my dad know and he will make it part of his daily routine to stop by and pray over her."

"Glenda, your parents are a blessing. I remember when I came home with you that one Christmas. If your parents saw anyone that seemed to be having a bad day or whatever, they took the time to pray for them. Watching them and the love they have in their hearts for everyone was so touching. It was a blessing I will never forget. Your parents mean the world to me."

"I will have to say, Liz, my parents go sowing seeds of love all the time. They are known wherever they go, but I wouldn't have it any other way. They keep telling me, I need to find a man and settle down. They are wanting grandchildren. I told them when I could find a man like my daddy, I would snatch him up. I think everybody here is looking. So far, I'm still single."

Both Liz and Glenda laughed.

Pulling in the parking garage, Liz felt at peace. It was as if she already knew Joanna was going to be transferred to Duke University. Getting on the elevator to go to her office, Chief Helton was getting off.

"Well, Liz, I just left your office. From the smile on your face, you must have some good news."

Liz's phone rang and it was Colleen.

"Hold on, Chief Helton. Let me take this call and then we can talk.

"Colleen, what have you found out?"

"Liz, can you and Chief Helton be here at the hospital around six this evening? Dr. Lucas will be able to talk to you both then."

Putting her hand over the phone, Liz asked Chief Helton if he could meet with Dr. Lucas and her at six at the hospital. He nodded yes.

"Colleen, that will be perfect. Thank you."

"So exactly what are we meeting this Dr. Lucas for?" asked Chief Helton.

"Remember when we talked and thought it might be best to move Joanna to another state? Well, this is what this meeting is all about. I have already contacted a place and hopefully we can have a conference call with the doctor in that state and get things moving."

"Well, I must say, Liz, you have certainly been busy. When we talked about this, I was hoping something like this could happen but had no idea it would happen so fast."

"Chief, nothing has happened yet; we are still in the talking stage. You have a few hours to do some serious praying, please don't let us down. See you at six."

With that Liz went to her office. She texted Glenda that a meeting was to take place at six at the hospital regarding Joanna. If she could have her doctor call around that time, she would have her phone on. Usually in meetings such as this, Liz turned her phone off.

Liz arrived at the hospital shortly before six and went to the fourth floor, where Chief Helton was already waiting.

"You didn't say where we were meeting so I came on up here."

"Colleen didn't say when she called, and I didn't ask. I assumed we would be meeting here in one of the rooms."

The door opened and Colleen walked out.

"If you two will follow me, I'll take you to what we call our conference room. We use it for a little bit of everything."

Walking down the hall passed the window where Joanna used to be, Liz 's heart began to break. If Joanna is moved away, she would not be able to come visit and pray over her, but if she did go to Duke, she knew Glenda's parents would be right there for that girl. Colleen led them to a room and said, "I'll let the doctor know you are here."

Chief Helton walked over and stood by the window, looking out.

Liz bowed her head and prayed.

"Dear Lord, you know this difficult situation. I am worried about what is going to happen. Please take these 'what ifs', help us to focus our thoughts on You and not worry about what could happen. Please lead and guide us and take control of this situation. Please, Lord, give us Your wisdom and give us peace. This meeting is for one of Your little children, that is relying on us to do what is best for her. I lift this meeting up to You in Your sweet and precious Holy name. Amen."

The door opened. Colleen and Dr. Lucas walked in. Once everyone was seated, Dr Lucas spoke up. In his hand was a folder full of papers. Liz knew they were medical records on Joanna. Closing her eyes to herself she said, "Okay Lord, this is all in Your hands."

As Dr. Lucas spoke, laying out all the records showing Joanna's progress, Liz's phone rang. They all looked up at her, for she knew all phones were to be on silence when in a meeting.

Taking her phone, Liz said, "Hello."

"Yes, this is Dr. Robert Warren from Duke University. Is this Liz Barnett?"

"Yes, Dr. Warren. I am so glad you have called. Can you hold please."

Placing her hand over the phone, Liz explained to Dr. Lucas, Colleen, and Chief Helton that this doctor could possibly help with the situation they were in with Joanna.

"Dr. Warren, I am going to place my phone on speaker so the others can hear what you have to say. In the room with me is Dr. Barry Lucas, Colleen Rivers a register nurse, Chief Craig Helton from the police department and myself."

"Wonderful, I will place you on speaker also, for with me is Glenda Felty, an attorney, Dr. Tad Reagan, Dr. Riley Cameron and Haley Simmons, a nurse practitioner."

"Dr. Warren, I assume Ms. Felty has filled you in on our conversation this afternoon." Liz said.

"Yes, she did. We would like to hear what Dr. Lucas has to say about the young lady in question."

Dr. Lucas began by asking Dr. Warren what he specialized in, the hospital he was affiliated with, and how he came to know about this case. They talked for about forty-five minutes, with the other doctors speaking up from time to time. After all questions were answered, then the doctors started discussing Joanna and her situation. From time to time, Colleen would fax the doctors' documents so they could look at what Dr. Lucas was discussing with them.

Glenda, Chief Helton, and Liz said very little during this time. The doctors used medical terminology in the discussion that they were not familiar with. The call lasted for nearly two hours. Finally, the doctors came to an agreement regarding Joanna.

Liz sat with tears in her eyes. She had prayed so hard over this case and now Joanna's future here had been decided. She asked Dr. Lucas if she could go see Joanna for few minutes. He gave her the usual ten minutes.

Colleen walked Liz back to Joanna's room, with neither saying a word. When Colleen opened the door for Liz, she said, "It's going to be okay." Then shut the door behind her.

Liz walked over to where Joanna laid. Taking the child's hand, Liz held it close to her. With tears running down her face, she prayed.

"Heavenly Father, giver of life and health, our comforter. Father, first of all, I want to thank You for hearing all our prayers. Tonight, Your mighty hand was in our presence. The decision that was made, we know was from Your guidance. We also acknowledge that your ways are higher than our ways and your thoughts are higher than our thoughts. In Romans 8:26-27: it says: *'In the same way, the Spirit helps us in our weakness. We do not know what we ought to pray for, but the Spirit himself intercedes for us through wordless groans. And he who searches our hearts knows the mind of the Spirit, because the Spirit intercedes for God's people in accordance with the will of God.* Thank You Father, for we know Joanna is in good hands. Amen."

Looking at Joanna, Liz leaned over and kissed her on the cheek. "I love you, Joanna. I couldn't love you anymore than if you were my own daughter. I gave you this name because it means 'God is gracious'. He has graciously healed your body and I know He will heal your mind. We are transporting you to another hospital where we know you will be safe, and you will have some awesome prayer warriors there praying over you every day. Glenda, my sweet friend, and her parents will become very dear to you. Her dad, Neal Felty is a pastor at a church there, and her mom, Doris Felty, well, I can't say enough about how wonderful they are. I will come and visit you ever chance I can, but I want you to know, I am still here for you. I'm not walking away. I wish so much; you could hear me and understand. I know deep down inside, one day I will get to see your beautiful eyes and smile. I'll be able to hug you and you can hug me back. I love you, Joanna."

Leaning over, Liz hugged her the best she could, then kissed her on the cheek. As she raised back up, she saw a twitch in Joanna's right hand. Putting her hand in hers, Liz said, "Joanna, if you can hear me, squeeze my hand if you possibly can."

Again, Joanna's fingers moved ever so slightly. The door opened and it was Colleen.

"Liz, time is up. We will let you come back to see her before she leaves."

"Colleen, her fingers on her right hand moved."

"Liz, it doesn't mean anything. The body twitches from time to time."

"No, Colleen. She can hear us; she is trying to communicate the best she can. This is a sign; she is going to be alright. God is healing her. Can't you see this?"

"Liz, I work in the medical field. I don't want to build up your hopes. She has been in a coma way too long. If she does wake up, I'm afraid she will be nothing more than a vegetable."

"I thought you had more faith than this. This is a sign, I know it. When she gets to Duke, she will wake up and with therapy, she is going to have a normal life."

"Liz, you are an attorney. Please don't get blindsided on this. You always have had a good head on your shoulders. Go home and get some rest. It will take several days to make all the arrangements on getting her transported. I will keep you posted; I promise."

Turning to walk out the door, Liz stopped and looked back at Joanna.

"I believe in you, Joanna. I know you can do this."

Walking to her car, Liz thought about all that had taken place. God had not only been present today, but He had answered so many prayers. She would never be able to thank Him enough.

"Dear Lord, You are a wonderful Savior. We are so unworthy of Your praise."

Through tears of joy, Liz managed to drive home.

Four days later, Colleen called Liz. "Joanna will be leaving this afternoon around one. If you want to say good-bye, you need to be here before twelve-thirty. After that, no one is permitted to go back with her. They will be preparing her for the helicopter flight to Duke."

"Thanks, Colleen, I'll do my best to be there."

Liz knew she was to be in court and was trying to figure out how to make it all work. She buzzed Dee to come into her office. Liz waited and still Dee had not come in, so she buzzed her again. Finally, she got up to go see if there was a problem. When she opened the door, Dee was on the phone, and she held up her hand for Liz to wait a minute. When she hung up the phone, she turned to Liz.

"Court has been canceled this morning at eleven-thirty; it has been rescheduled till next week. Sorry, I couldn't come into your office when you buzzed, but I was trying to get this scheduled."

"Dee, that's what I was going to talk to you about. This is perfect. God has come through again for me. I need to be at the hospital before twelve-thirty." Walking over to Dee, Liz gave her a hug. "What would I ever do without you."

At twelve Liz texted Colleen that she was at the hospital. She waited and waited, then began to wonder if something was wrong. Finally, Colleen came out to Liz.

"Sorry to keep you waiting, Liz, but we are making sure we have copies of everything she will need. Dr. Lucas and I will be on the helicopter with her just in case something might go wrong."

"I totally understand. How is she doing today? Do you think she understands she is being moved?"

"Dr. Lucas and I both have tried to explain to her what is going on, how much she is able to retain, we are not sure. We told her we would be with her, and she had nothing to fear. We received no response."

"May I see her now?"

"Sure. Liz, you won't be able to stay long. I know you want to pray over her, and that's good, but know you are limited on time."

Liz walked into the room where Joanna laid. Taking her hand, Liz could feel tears forming in her eyes. She needed strength, for telling this sweet child bye broke her heart.

"Joanna, it's me, Liz. You are getting ready to go to another hospital where they can help you even more than they can here. You will be safe and will have many new friends that will care and love you. I hope you will be able to remember some of the scripture I have read to you and some of the prayers I have prayed over you. Even though I won't be able to see you every day, I want you to know, I will still be praying for you.

"Dear Heavenly Father, I come before You for You are the great healer, and I place my trust in Your loving hands. Father, I pray that You give Joanna the strength to endure and the courage to face each day. Pour Your healing grace upon her body, mind and spirit. Lord it says in Psalm 30:2. *'Lord my God, I called to You for help, and You healed me'. Joanna is not able to call to You, so on her behalf, I ask that You heal her. In my heart Lord, I remember Palms 91. Protect her, Father, and protect those that are on this flight to North Carolina. Be with those waiting her arrival, be with each person that has contact with her, that they have the love of God in their heart, and she will be able to feel it. Father, I pray again for love, peace, joy, strength, health and continued healing for Joanna. I thank You so much, for bringing her into my life. I love her and I pray she will feel the wonderful love You have for her, for there is no greater love, than the love of our precious Lord and Savior. Bless her in a very special way, for she has had to endure so much. I lift her up to You. Amen."*

Colleen opened the door. "Liz, they are ready for her."

With tears in her eyes, Liz leaned over to hug Joanna and kiss her on the forehead. She whispered in Joanna's ears.

"You are going to pull through this. The next time I see you, you will be up walking, and you will be able to talk to me. I believe that with all my heart. Don't give up. Keep fighting, for I know you can do it."

Colleen then rolled Joanna out the door, for her flight to North Carolina.

<h1 style="text-align:center">Eight</h1>

aturday morning, Liz got up early to catch up on some things before Millie and her friends arrived. She felt guilty not working at the shelter. It seemed like someone else was always having to cover for her. Looking at her watch, she knew they would be there soon. As Sandy and Myra came in, Millie was right behind them.

Greeting each other with a big hug, Liz asked, "So you are alone. I was expecting you to have someone with you."

"I do. They are at the coffee shop a few blocks down. Are you ready?"

"So, how many are waiting on us at the coffee shop?" Liz asked.

"Liz, do you always have to ask so many questions? Just relax and enjoy the day."

"Millie, I could relax if I knew what you had in the works. What are you planning, or should I say scheming?"

"You will just have to wait and see. Are you ready?"

"Almost, I need to go over a few things with Sandy and Myra, then I will be ready, I think!"

Not knowing what Millie was up to, Liz began to think it might have been better to stay home. Going over things with Sandy and Myra, she thanked them for working for her over the weekend, then out the door she went with Millie, wondering what she was getting herself into.

Coming upon the coffee shop, Millie was grinning from ear to ear. Turning to Liz, she said, "Please be on your best behavior and don't start out dissecting everything."

"Millie, what are you talking about?"

"You know how you attorneys are. You can't just have a conversation and relax; you have to dissect very word that is said. So, this weekend, forget you are an attorney, be like most people."

"Millie, you are in the medical field. When someone has an ache or pain, what do you do?"

"Okay, point taken, but please try and relax."

Walking into the coffee shop, Millie went straight to a table where two men were sitting. Both men stood when they neared the table.

"Hey, guys, I would like for you to meet my cousin, Liz. Liz, this is Scott Hunter and his brother Steve Hunter."

Smiling, Liz said, "Scott and I have met before. How are you doing?"

"Fine, Ms. Barnett. Millie had mentioned her cousin to me, but I had no idea it was you. It's so good to see you again."

"Please, call me Liz."

Millie spoke up. "When did you two meet?"

Scott said, "Ms. Barnett, I mean Liz, represented a good friend of mine a few years ago. She is an excellent attorney. I told her if I ever needed one, I would definitely keep her in mind."

"Small world. Liz, do you know Steve, too?" asked Millie.

"No, don't think I have seen him my courtroom."

With that, they all laughed.

Steve held out his hand to shake hands with Liz.

"It's a pleasure to meet you and I hope to stay out of your courtroom, but should I find myself there, I hope we are on the same side."

Before they realized it, they had spent over two hours in the coffee shop. Millie then decided they should walk around and see places in Nashville. The day was so beautiful and sunny, with just a slight breeze. Bicentennial Park was close by, so they saw the two-hundred-foot granite map of the state, a World War II Memorial, a 95-Bell Carillon along with many other sites. Soon, the smell of food overtook them, and they needed to find a place to rest from all the walking they had done.

After dinner, Millie drove them around to different sites and then they headed back to drop Liz off at her place. When Liz mentioned church on Sunday morning, the guys were all for going and said they would see her at church. Liz had to admit, the day had been a great day. She had not thought about work, Joanna, or the shelter. It had really been such a relaxing day and one that she needed. When she thought Millie had had time to drop the guys off at their hotel, she texted her.

"Are you at your parents yet?"

"Yes, want to talk?" was Millie's reply.

Hitting the speed button, Liz called Millie.

"Well, Liz, what do you think about today?"

"Millie, I will have to say, this morning I was having second thoughts about going, but I'm so glad I did."

"Well, I think you and Steve hit it off pretty good. You two never seem to run out of anything to talk about."

"You know, when I met Scott, I never thought of ever seeing him again, and I had no idea he had a brother. I do remember telling him about you, and maybe your paths might cross at Duke. Looks like they did."

"So, what do you think about Steve?" Millie asked.

"He is very nice, but Millie, he lives in North Carolina. I'm not into long-distance relations."

"Liz, you two seem to have so much in common. Give things a chance."

"He is a doctor and is studying under some professor to advance in his career. I'm sure he doesn't have time for a long-distance relationship, and I know I don't want to move to North Carolina. We had a good time, he is a great guy, but he's not for me. I appreciate what you are trying to do, but I'm okay. Someday the right guy will come along, but now is not the time."

"Liz, I wish you would give Steve a chance. You might be passing up a good thing."

"Millie, I'm leaving it in the hands of God. He knows what is best. It's been a long but good day, so I'll see everyone at church tomorrow."

"Good night, Liz. Know, I'm praying for you."

As Liz lay in bed, she thought about the day. Steve was a nice guy and if he lived in Nashville, she might consider him, but with him in North Carolina, she refused to even think about it."

After church they went over to Roy and Debbie Barnett's for a cookout. Debbie was so happy that Millie had finally found a guy that they approved of. She asked Liz, "So what do you think of Steve?"

"Aunt Debbie, he is nice, but he lives in North Carolina. I'm in Nashville."

"But honey, you and Millie could be like your mom and me. We married brothers."

"Aunt Debbie, you also lived in the same town. You two grew up together. This is all you and Mom have ever known. I don't want a long-distance relationship and I have no desire to move. It's not the same as it was with you, Mom, Dad, and Uncle Roy."

"I understand what you're saying, but I also know you two seem to have a certain chemistry between you."

"You sound like Millie, playing matchmaker. Thanks, but I'm going to pass."

After church that night, the four went out for coffee and then Liz said her goodbyes. She was not able to take Monday off, despite Millie's protest, and didn't want to admit to anyone that she liked Steve, especially to Millie.

Liz had taken her shower and was getting ready for bed when her phone rang. Thinking it was Millie, she said, "Yes."

"Liz, Chief Helton here. When did you start answering your phone that way?"

"Oh, Chief. Sorry, I thought you were someone else and didn't look to see who was calling."

"Not a problem, but I do have some news for you. We know who our mystery man is."

"That is wonderful. How did you find out?" Liz asked.

"A friend of mine from Alabama gave me a call. It seems they have been looking for him also. When our men were searching the database trying to match fingerprints, Captain Malcom Tilson was notified by one of his men about the possible match. He gave me a call. We talked for a while and compared notes. It seems our mystery man is Clarence Walters. Several years ago, his wife was found by a neighbor, badly beaten. She was rushed to the hospital but later died. The neighbor said they hadn't seen Mr. Walters for several days or their daughter. The child's name was Carrie. She was about six years old then. Captain Tilson had a picture of the child and faxed it to me. Our team here took the picture and advanced it to the age fifteen and guess what? We think Carrie is your Joanna."

Nothing but silence. Liz did not respond to what Captain Helton had said.

"Liz, are you still there?"

"Yes, I'm here, trying to take in all that you just said. I'm so glad we had her transferred to another place and gave her a new name. What about any family they may have had?"

"The neighbors stated they never saw anyone visit them. As for any family, they never heard Mrs. Walters or Carrie speak of any. They said Mr. Walters would nod when he saw them, but never spoke to them. They considered him a strange man. Also, if the little girl or her mother was outside when he came home, they all went inside."

"So how do you know this man is the one who left the young girl at my door.? Do they have a picture of him?'"

"Captain Tilson had the neighbor to look at the picture we had on our database, and they identified him. Also, he had a set of prints from inside the house where they lived that matched ours perfectly.”

“How long have you known about all this, Chief?” Liz asked.

“Friday evening, I received his call and we have been working back and forth ever since. Little by little the pieces started falling into place. I knew you had plans for the weekend and didn’t want to bother you.”

“I appreciate this, but when it comes to Joanna, I want to know everything.”

“I feel she is safe, but I worry about you. She was left at your doorstep. He has no idea if she is still alive or has passed. He may come after you for answers,” replied Chief Helton.

“I will be okay. I have the monitor on, and you keep close check on that. I do wonder what name he is going by now and if Joanna has been in school. Still, so many unanswered questions.”

“He may come snooping around again, trying to find her. If so, I want to be notified immediately. Well, that’s all I have for now. Get some rest, and I’ll be talking to you more.”

“Good night, Chief, and thanks for the information.”

Nine

Early the next morning, Liz's phone rang. She had just stepped out of the shower. Not recognizing the number, she was unsure if she should answer it. She let it go to voice mail instead and discovered the caller was Steve Hunter. She hadn't given him her number, so he must have gotten it from Millie. Before she could call him back, her phone rang again, and it was the same number. This time she answered it.

"Hello."

"Liz, good morning. This is Steve. I hope I haven't called too early?"

"No, I was up. Is everything alright?"

"Yes, yes. I didn't mean to alarm you. I had asked Millie for your number, and I hope you don't mind."

"No, that's fine. I wasn't expecting to hear from you this morning and I was afraid something was wrong when I heard your voice mail. I don't think you realized it, but all I heard you say, 'I must have dialed the wrong number.'"

"Oh, I'm sorry. When you didn't answer, I was telling Scott, I thought I had dialed the number wrong, unaware it was recording my conversation. Please forgive me."

"No worries. Are you guys on your way back to North Carolina?"

"We will be soon. Waiting on Millie. She stayed at her parents' house last night. I'm sure they are keeping her with them for as long as they can. They are really nice folks. Your parents are nice also. I think it's great they were friends from grade school on, then got married, have a business together, and live next door to each other. I can see why you and Millie are so close."

"Yes, we are more like sisters than cousins. How about you and Scott? Think you two might ever open up a practice together?"

"Not sure. We are both doctors, but practice in different fields. Who knows what is ahead for us? Anyway, the reason I called, I wanted you to know what a wonderful time I had this weekend and wondered if you would mind me calling you from time to time?"

Liz wasn't sure how to answer. She really liked Steve, but he lived in another state. Maybe he just wanted to be friends and she was reading more into this than what was there. Millie always said she had a bad habit of doing this.

"Sure, Steve, that would be great. I will say this, the evenings are the best time to reach me and then that's a hit or miss."

"Don't worry, Liz, evenings would be the only time I could call. I'm at the hospital some mornings around five and don't get home till seven, maybe eight."

"My, you do have long hours. Do you ever sleep?" she asked.

"This is of my own doing. I'm studying under a professor that is so knowledgeable and he has taken me under his wing. You can learn so much from textbooks, but hands-on is where you truly learn, and he is the best. Not everyone gets the opportunity to work by his side. I consider it a blessing from God for this is something I have always wanted to do."

"Steve, this is wonderful. I am so happy for you, and I'm sure you are going to be outstanding in your career."

"I won't keep you and sorry I have talked so long for I know you are getting ready for work. When I have a free minute one evening, I'll give you a call, and again, I really enjoyed this weekend. Have a blessed day."

"Thanks, Steve, you, too."

Hanging up the phone, Liz didn't know what to make of his call. She was so sure he would not want a long-distance relationship, especially with his studies. Why would he want to keep in touch? She would have to think about this another time; she was eager to get to work to see if Chief Helton had any new information. Liz went into the kitchen and found that Jana already had the coffee on and blueberry muffins made.

"How is the morning going so far, Jana?" Liz asked.

"So far, so good. We do have a full house already today. Some went home last week and here we are full again. It's a shame some women have to look for safety, then it's good we are here for them. The stories some of those women tell will break your heart."

"I know, Jana, but like you said, we can offer them a safe place to stay until they can work things out or decide where they need to go. Well, I'm off to work. If you need me, give me a call, and if not, I'll see you tonight."

As soon as Liz arrived at work, she went by Chief Helton's office. He was out on a call. She went to her office and found a stack of papers on her desk to read, so she settled in and got started. Dee popped her head in about thirty minutes later.

"Morning. Liz. You are here early. Care for a cup of fresh-brewed coffee?"

"Dee, that would be wonderful. Looks like you were busy Friday, or did you work Saturday?"

"No, I stayed late Friday. I have a copy of this week's schedule for you on your desk to your right. Did you have fun this weekend with Millie?"

"Yes, I did."

"Did she bring anyone with her?" Dee asked.

"Yes, she brought some friends that she works with. That's a good drive and I'm sure she didn't want to make the drive alone. Oh, if Chief Helton comes by, I would like to see him."

"I don't think he will be in today. I heard one of the officers on the elevator say something that the Chief was headed to Alabama today. Not sure if it's for a case or he has family there."

"That's odd, I spoke to him last night and he never said anything about going to Alabama today!"

Liz began to wonder what he was up to and why he never mentioned it to her when they talked. He always wanted her to be up front with him and not keep anything from him, yet he didn't always share his information with her or at least all of it. This was going to be addressed when he came back in.

At the end of the day, Liz still had heard nothing from Chief Helton. Although she wanted so much to know what was going on, she knew she had to wait until he got back. Hopefully, he had more information or maybe they had subpoenaed this Mr.

Walters. At least Joanna was safe, and when she got home, she would call and check on her.

Nina and Jana both were busy in the kitchen, for like Jana had said that morning, they had a full house.

"Evening, ladies. What can I do to help?" Liz asked.

"Liz, we have enough volunteers helping here in the kitchen, if you could answer that phone, it would be a blessing. It has rung almost non-stop today," was Nina's reply.

"I can certainly do that," said Liz. "I will be in the office if you need me."

Liz knew she had some paperwork to address in her office in addition to manning the phone. About an hour later, Nina walked in.

"Has that phone rung at all since you have been in here?"

"No, Nina, it hasn't. Not one call."

"Well, it did today. Started about ten this morning and never stopped."

"Was it all about women needing a place to stay, Nina?" Liz asked.

"Some, but not all. We did receive one strange call. Some guy called and asked if we took in abused men. Said he had nowhere to go and desperately needed a place for a few days. I gave him Pastor Dotson's number and told him he could help him, that this was for women only. Then he asked if he could stay at least one night, and I told him to call Pastor Dotson. The man was not very happy with me to say the least, and I haven't had a chance to follow up to see if he called our pastor."

"Nina, by any chance, did his voice sound familiar to you in any way?"

"Sorry, Liz. A lady had just come in. She had a baby with her, and they were both crying. Realizing I couldn't help the man, I referred him to Rod and didn't give it much thought. Why do you ask?"

"Chief Helton thinks he knows who Joanna's dad is and has some other information. We are almost sure the man looking for Carrie is after our Joanna. I was wondering - if this man - might be this guy and it was his way of getting in here to look around."

"I hadn't thought of that. As you know, he came here wanting to look around to see if his daughter was here and wasn't happy when he was refused. This may be another way of trying to get in. Oh, that is sneaky."

"Don't worry Nina, no harm has been done. You did the right thing. Think I will call Pastor Rod and see if he has received any such call. This is all very interesting."

"Liz, have you heard how Joanna is doing? Do you think she will ever wake up? She has been in a coma for a very long time."

"No, Nina, I haven't called them today. Was going to check on her tonight, but first I'm going to call Pastor Rod. When I hear from both, I'll let you know. Oh, thanks for telling me about that phone call."

"I wish I had been more in tune to the caller. I'll try to do better the next time. Whenever you are ready, your dinner is waiting on you."

"Thanks, Nina. Let me makes these calls and I'll be right in."

Calling Pastor Rod, Liz wondered if this was Clarence Walters still trying to get in to see Joanna.

"God Bless, this is Pastor Dotson,"

"Pastor Rod, this is Liz, how are you doing this evening?"

"Liz, I am doing great. To what do I owe the pleasure of this call?"

"Is this a good time to talk or are you in the middle of something?"

"No, I'm free to talk. What's on your mind?" he asked.

"Here at the shelter today, some man called looking for a place to stay for at least a few nights. Nina gave him your name and number. We were wondering if he had called you?"

"No, Liz, no one has called needing a place to stay. All my calls today have been regarding someone in the hospital, nursing home, or has passed."

"That's what I thought," Liz replied. "But wanted to follow up and make sure. I didn't think this guy was on the up and up with Nina."

"Liz, a thought just crossed my mind. That young girl we have been praying for, do you think by any chance it was the man that left her at your door?"

"Rod, that is exactly what we are thinking. At least she is safe from him now."

"What about you, Liz? Do you feel safe?"

"Chief Helton keeps close tabs on me. Trust me. Thank you for your time, Rod, and thank you for all your prayers for this young girl. Our church has been a huge blessing not only to me, but to so many people. Couldn't make without you."

"No, Liz, we couldn't make it without God. His love is so phenomenal. We need to keep working on being more like Him."

"You are so right. We all fall so short every day. The good thing is, no matter how short we fall, He still loves us unconditionally. Thanks again for your help, Rod. See you Sunday."

Hanging up the phone, Liz was almost certain the man calling that afternoon was the man looking for Joanna. Why was he so eager to find her if he left her for dead at her door? Liz was lost in her thoughts when her cell phone rang. It was from Duke University.

"Hello, this is Liz Barnett.

"Miss Barnett, this is Dr. Robert Warren, from Duke University. How are you this evening?"

"Dr. Warren, I am fine and you?"

"Doing wonderful. I'm calling about our patient Joanna. Wanted to give you an update on her since she has been here. I am pleased to say we feel she is making some progress. We have noticed more twitching in her hands, and she is making more sounds, not the same groaning sounds. All of this is a positive."

"Dr. Warren, I noticed a twitching in her hand before she left, and the nurse here said that was from her body and not her actually trying to move her hand. So do you feel this is Joanna trying to respond?"

"We have monitored her very closely. We feel she is trying to move her hands. Also, the sounds she is making is like someone trying to say something. We have had other cases where a person is in a coma, so we know more what to look for and to hear, and this is what we are seeing in her. Now, when she will wake up, I have no idea. I will say this, a Preacher Neal Felty has been stopping by every day. He prays over so many of our patients, he, and his wife Doris. Today while he was here, he mentioned your name when speaking to Joanna. He noticed a small tear down the side of her face. Thought you would want to know this."

Liz could feel her own tears. Oh, how she wanted to see Joanna and give her a hug.

"Dr. Warren, this is great news. I'm so glad you have called. Anything else about that sweet girl?"

"No, I wanted to give you an update on her, and next week, someone else maybe giving you a call. There are several doctors working on her case, and you may be hearing from one of them. You have a blessed evening, Miss Barnett."

Liz sat in her chair with her eyes closed and kept saying over and over, "Thank You, Lord. Thank You so much for cradling that child in Your loving arms."

Nina walked in and saw Liz.

"Liz, are you okay? What's wrong?"

"Oh, Nina, I just got off the phone with a doctor at Duke where Joanna is. Both her hands are twitching, and she is making different sounds."

"Liz, that is wonderful."

"The best part, Pastor Felty, my friend Glenda's dad, is going by to pray with her. He mentioned my name to Joanna, and they saw a tear roll down the side of her face. Nina, she can hear, and she is trying to wake up. She is going to make; I know she is."

Nina reached out to hug Liz. They both cried and lifted up a word of thanks.

"Liz, this is a blessing. God is hearing our prayers."

"I also spoke to Rod. No one called him today for a place to stay."

"So it was that man, still trying to get in here. Well, he can try all he wants, but God has his angels around that child. I hope they find him and beat him like he did that poor girl. He deserves every lick."

Liz looked at Nina. "That's not being God like!"

"I'm sorry, Liz. Sometimes the ole devil slips right out of me. That poor girl didn't deserve what he did to her, and I feel it's only right he receives the same treatment except no one to help him. He can just lay there in agony and think about what he has done."

"What if he wants to find her and apologize and ask for forgiveness?"

"Liz, we will cross that bridge if it should happen. I'm not going to hold my breath, either. By the way, you need to eat. I'll go reheat your food."

Liz could hear Nina mumbling as she went down the hall. Deep down inside, she had to agree with Nina. That man deserved a severe punishment.

Ten

hief Helton was gone almost all week. When he finally came back into work, he stopped by Liz's office. "Hey, Liz, got a minute?"

"Well, Chief, did you finally decide to come back to work?"

"I have been working, Liz. It just so happened I was able to add in a little relaxation."

"In Alabama?"

"Yes, in Alabama. I went down to see Captain Malcom Tilson. Remember, he is the one I was telling you that had called me."

"But why couldn't you have discussed the case over the phone? What are you keeping from me?"

"Malcom and I go way back. We have been friends since childhood. I went down and stayed with him and his family, plus did some investigating on our Joanna case."

"I wondered why you didn't send someone else to investigate the case." Liz said. "Sometimes it's hard to pass up an opportunity to visit with an old friend and work also."

"Malcom is good at his job. Not much escapes him. We met in the sixth grade and stayed close friends all through school. Then we decided to go into law enforcement. That guy can shoot. I would say he is still the best. He has been offered some outstanding jobs, but he stays right there in his little town, content as could be."

"Is he from Alabama?" Liz asked.

"Yes, and so am I. That's another reason I wanted to go."

"I didn't know you were from Alabama. I always thought you were from here in Nashville! What brought you here?"

"My wife. What can I say."

"That's a good reason. Did she not want to move to Alabama?"

"I came here for my sister's wedding. My wife had become my sister's best friend and was in the wedding. I was in the wedding also. My sister introduced us, I was love struck and end of story."

"I knew your wife and sister were close but didn't know the story behind it. I will say you made a very wise choice. You married a very sweet lady, landed a good job, and you have the privilege of working with someone as awesome as me. What more could you want?"

Chief Helton only shook his head at Liz's comment.

"So, when are you going to settle down, Liz? Did Millie bring home anyone interesting?"

"She brought home two friends that she works with. It was good that she did, that way she had someone to help with the drive and keep her company. Now, back to your trip to Alabama!"

"Changing the subject, huh?"

"No, I have a meeting soon and I want to know what you found out."

"It seems this Clarence Walters is the man that has been snooping around looking for Carrie, or Joanna. Malcom took me to where they use to live. The same people still lived next to that house. We went over everything with them that Malcom and others had questioned them on. This time the house that Walters lived in was empty. The back door was not locked so we went in. We took each room and went over it with a fine-toothed comb. Couldn't find a thing that would give any clues. As we walked out the back door, a trash can was on the porch full of junk. Malcom pulled out a picture. The glass was broken, and the frame bent. The picture was of a dog. He decided to look on the back of the picture, hoping to see if someone had written anything. Did we ever get a surprise? Behind the picture was a picture of Walters, Carrie, and her mom. They were very young, for Carrie looked to be about four years old. The picture was in bad shape, so Malcom took it to a guy he knew to work on it."

"Oh, Chief, I want to look at the picture when you get it. It was meant to find that picture in the trash. It's a shame the neighbors couldn't be of more help."

"It seems Mrs. Walters and the girl came out of the house very little. We did question them about a dog, and they said there was a dog for a while but like the others, you saw very little of it. Apparently, Carrie never got to go to school. They think her mom may have homeschooled her."

"Chief, did they say what Joanna's mother's name was? Also, calling her Carrie seems awkward to me, it's easier for me to refer to her as Joanna."

"Got it. Malcom referrers to her as Carrie, you call her Joanna. Think I'll call her Carrie Joanna, that way everyone gets the name. No, the neighbors only refer to her as Mrs. Walters. Sometimes the mail carrier would put the mail in the wrong box, and that's how they found out his name was Clarence Walters. They heard Mrs. Walters call the child Carrie. Mr. Walters referred to his wife as, woman."

"That's strange. Why would he not call her by her name? Did you check for a marriage certificate? That would have both names and a birth certificate for Joanna."

"Malcom already checked on a marriage certificate and found nothing. We both are doing some checking on Carrie Joanna for a birth certificate."

Tapping the desk with her pen, Liz said, "I wonder if they were ever married, which would explain no marriage certificate. Maybe Joanna's name is under her mother's maiden name, whatever that is."

"Good point, Liz. Hadn't thought about the child not having Walters for a last name. Just when I think we are getting somewhere, the hole gets deeper."

"Chief, we must uncover every rock. Joanna may have family that would love to have her, take her in, and give her a good home. She deserves it."

"No argument there. Well, that's all the news, now, back to the drawing board."

"Before you go, Chief, there is something you might want to know."

"I hope it's good news. We certainly could use it. What have you got?"

"About a week ago, Nina, one of the workers at the shelter, received a call from a man that was needing a place to stay for a few days. Said he had been abused and had nowhere to go."

Leaning forward in his chair. Chief Helton looked at Liz.

"Did he come to the shelter?"

"No. He called. Nina gave him Pastor Rod Dotson's name and phone number and told him our place was for women only and that Pastor Dotson would be able to help him. The man never called Pastor Dotson."

"How do you know for sure he didn't call?"

"Pastor Rod Dotson is our pastor and I called him when she told me about the phone call. He said no one had called that day needing a place to stay or needing protection from anyone."

"So, our Mr. Walters is still trying to get inside your place. He just won't give up will he? Liz, do not remove that monitor from your body. We already have cameras and alarms set up. Do you still have a guard twenty-four seven at your house?"

"Yes. The guys are great. Every morning, someone walks me to my car. When I arrive here, I park in front of the elevator and when that door opens, an officer is there. The only privacy I have is when I take a shower. That's the only time the monitor is not on me."

"Wonder if that monitor is waterproof? I wouldn't want you to get shocked while showering."

"Really, Chief."

Getting up to leave, Chief Helton said, "You realize, if we don't catch this man, you will be wearing that monitor for the rest of your life."

Smiling, he walked out the door.
Liz raised her head slightly and just looked at him.

Eleven

Millie and Scott got together as much as possible. His schedule was packed, but he always found time to call her, if only for a few minutes, and if he had any extra time to spare, he would stop by to see her. Scott was so different than Alex. She often wondered what she ever saw in Alex. Scott was a very positive person. He saw good in everything. She was amazed at how he treated his patients. If he had bad news to give them, before he left the room, he made sure they were lifted up. He even prayed with most of them. She felt God outdid himself with Scott. He was handsome, had a wonderful personality, very loving, kind, caring, and how happy she felt when he would give her a hug. He treated her the way any parent would want a man to treat their daughter. The one thing he would never do, and that was discuss his patients with her. If she happened to be in the room working with one of his patients and he came in, what she witnessed was all she knew. He was very private about his patients; he treated each one with the upmost respect. He was more than a family doctor and had mentioned about studying more in a specialty field like Steve. She had no idea what Steve was studying, for Scott never talked about it. He felt what his brother wanted to be was his choice. If Steve was as committed to his work as Scott, then he was one fine doctor.

On Millie's day off, she decided at the last-minute to drop by Glenda's. She always enjoyed talking to her. Like Scott, she had a way of making everything seem so much better. She was pleased to find Glenda at home.

"Millie, so good to see you. Come in." said Glenda.

"Sorry to drop by without calling first, but I have the day off and thought about you."

"Millie, you are welcome here anytime. So, tell me, how are things going with you?"

"Couldn't be better. I have tried to call Liz a few times this week, and she has been in court or with a client. When she calls me back, then I'm not able to talk."

"Millie, you seem very happy and relaxed. Your smile is contagious. So, who is responsible for the glow of yours?"

"Is it that obvious?"

"Yes. So, who is the lucky guy?"

"He is a doctor at Duke where I work. Oh, Glenda, he is absolutely wonderful. He has it all. You name it and that's him."

"Millie, this is good news. So, how serious are things between you two?"

"Oh, we are just dating. He is thinking about going back to school and advancing in his career. He's a family practitioner and enjoys his work but is thinking about being a specialist. He has a brother who is a doctor also but studying to be a specialist."

"Are they not going into the same field?" Glenda asked.

"I have no idea what his brother is studying for. Their work is something they don't talk about. Liz even went out with his brother, and he never told her."

"Millie, did you say Liz went out on a date?"

"Well, she would say it wasn't a date. I went home a few weeks ago and the two brothers went with me. I stayed at my parents, and they got a hotel."

"So how did Liz get involved in this?"

"I was trying to play matchmaker. Steve, Scott's brother, is handsome also. Those guys don't fall short on anything. Anyway, I was hoping Liz might take a liking to him and vice versa but nothing. Her excuse was, she didn't want a long-distance relationship. Glenda, you should have seen those two. I'm telling you; they are made for each other, and I don't know how to make them see this."

"Now, Millie, if it's meant, it will work out. You need to pray about it. Besides, if he is still in school, he may want to wait until he has his schooling behind him. This way he can focus solely on his studies."

"I guess you're right, I just want to help Liz out. She never shows an interest in any man. Do you ever date, Glenda?"

"Some. Like Liz, I'm picky. Being an attorney and having this shelter makes you really look at things. I am seeing a guy but taking my time also."

"So, how do you work him into your busy schedule? I know this place can snatch up any free time you may have."

"I actually hired a man and his wife to run my shelter. It's still mine and I oversee things. Having them gives me some freedom that I didn't have before."

"Oh, Glenda, I don't think Liz would let someone run her place."

"I have spoken to Liz about this. In fact, I ran it by her before I made my decision. This couple has no family. They have traveled with their work all their lives, made a good living, and wanted to settle down. Then they realized retirement wasn't what they thought it would be. I met them through a client of mine. They were what I needed, and I had what they were looking for. God orchestrated it perfectly. I moved out, moved back into my old room at my parents', and now I'm here when I want to be."

"Liz has delegated some things, but she is still over it all. When you spoke to her, what was her reaction?"

"She thought it was a great idea. You see, when I met Mr. and Mrs. Toppins, I met them regarding something else. While we were talking, I received a call about something at the shelter. Overhearing some of my conversation, Mrs. Toppins asked about the shelter. I explained to her how it all came about. She was so excited because she had never heard of a place like this and questioned me more. A few days later, she called me and ask if I would consider letting her and her husband work there and take care of whatever came about. I gave it some thought, talked it over with a few people, did some praying and have not regretted this decision. Mr. and Mrs. Toppins are a blessing from God. Speaking of them, here they are."

Glenda stood when the couple walked in and so did Millie.

"Millie, I want you to meet Ralph and Rosy Toppins. They are my blessing from God that I was telling you about. Ralph, Rosy, this is my dear friend, Millie Barnett."

They each shook hands.

Millie said, "Glenda tells me what a wonderful job you both are doing here at the shelter."

"Finding this place was an answer to a prayer." Rosy replied. "We love it here and enjoy so much what we are doing."

"Yes, Glenda came into our lives at the perfect time. We were living in a hotel at the time and had not yet decided on a house to buy. This solved many decisions we were trying to make. We now have a place to live and doing God's work. We feel so blessed and had no idea so many women were in need." said Ralph Toppins.

"May I add, they are perfect for this job," replied Glenda. "God was hearing prayers from both of us and brought it all together. He is so good."

Millie spoke up. "Yes, God is very good. I know from first-hand experience what He can do for you."

"Don't mean to rush off, but we have a few things to do. It was so nice to meet you, Millie. Come by any time and see us."

"Mr. and Mrs. Toppins, it was a pleasure to meet you, and I will try to stop by again soon."

"Oh, Millie, call us Ralph and Rosy. We are friends now and don't need to be so formal."

Rosy gave Millie a hug and they walked away.

"Glenda, I really like them. They are a jewel."

"Millie, everyone that meets them falls in love with them. That's one of the reasons I hired them. Maybe Liz will be fortunate enough to find her a Ralph and Rosy."

"That would be awesome. We can pray for that, also, that she will find an interest in Steve."

"Why are you so set on this Steve guy for Liz?"

"I'm sure you know that our parents are brothers and sisters. My mom and Liz's mom are sisters, and my dad and Liz's dad are brothers. If things worked out for Scott and me and then things worked out for Liz and Steve, it would almost be the same thing, only Liz and I are cousins, not sisters, but we were raised as if we were sisters."

"Millie, you need to let Liz and Steve make their own decisions about this. I understand what you are saying, and in your mind, it would be the perfect solution, but in reality, are they meant for each other?"

"Glenda, if you could have seen them together a few weeks ago, you would know what I'm trying to say. They both are so hung up in their work, that they can't see how suited they are for each other."

"Still, Millie, let God take care of this. If it is meant for them to be together, God will make a way and when the time is right."

"I know you're right Glenda. But it doesn't hurt to wish."

"You mean it doesn't hurt to pray. You have got to give it to God."

"Okay. This is what I love about you, Glenda. I have missed talking to you. You help me put things where they need to be."

"Millie, God put Liz and me as roommates for a reason years ago. He knew what was ahead and He was laying everything out. Before I left for college, my family and I prayed that I would have a godly roommate and He delivered. I couldn't have asked for a better one. This is why I'm saying, give this about Liz and Steve to God. He has something in store for them, and we must wait and see what glorious thing He has coming."

"I had better go, I have stayed longer now than I had planned. Glenda, it has been so good to see and talk to you. To me, you are a special blessing. I love you."

Millie hugged Glenda.

"Millie, call or come by anytime. You are always welcome, and you know I love you, too."

Millie knew Glenda was right.. As much as she wanted Steve and Liz to get together, she needed to pray and leave it up to God.

Twelve

ourth of July was a few days away and Millie would be coming in. Liz wondered if she would be bringing Scott and Steve with her. Part of her hoped she would and then another part hoped she didn't. She still was uncertain about her feelings for Steve. If only he lived in Nashville, this would make things so much easier. As she sat pondering over the Fourth, her phone rang. It was from Duke Hospital.

Liz, grab up her phone, "Hello."

"Is this Liz Barnett?"

"Yes, it is," she replied.

"Ms. Barnett, this is Dr. Riley Cameron, from Duke Hospital. How are you today?"

"Dr. Cameron, I'm doing fine. How is Joanna doing? Any improvements?"

"That's why I'm calling. Our Joanna opened her eyes today."

"She did? Oh, that is wonderful. Was she able to speak?"

"No, she only opened her eyes and moved them as if looking around. She didn't turn her head any, but I'm guessing they were open about five minutes and then closed. Her hands have been twitching a little more, as well as her feet. These are all good signs, and I knew you would be pleased to hear this."

"Oh, Dr. Cameron, this is what I have been praying for. I knew she would wake up one day."

"Ms. Barnett, she didn't actually wake up. Opening her eyes is a good sign, she still has a way to go. But everything that she does is an improvement. We will take whatever progress she can give."

"I understand, she has been like this for so long and I want her to wake up and have a normal life."

"Ms. Barnett, you do realize, that if and when Joanna wakes up, she won't be the same. Being in a coma for as long as she has been, she may have brain damage."

"I realize all this, Dr. Cameron, but as long as there is the tiniest hope of her making a full recovery, I'm hanging on to that. I'm not giving up on that girl. She has fought too hard to be where she is now."

"We, here at Duke, don't want you to be disappointed if her recovery is not what you're looking for. We are doing all we can, and the rest is up to her."

"This is where I will have to disagree with you, Dr. Cameron. Her recovery is also up to God, and I believe with all my heart, Joanna will pull through this. God has something special in store for her, I just know it. But thank you so much for the update and wonderful news. You have made my day. I'm looking forward to your next call."

"Ms. Barnett, you have a blessed day. We will talk again soon."

Liz was so excited. She had so many people to call and share the news about Joanna, but first things first. Bowing her head, she gave thanks to God."

Early Saturday morning, Millie called Liz.

"Good morning, Liz, are you ready for the Fourth?"

"Morning, Millie. I'm ready. What time do you think you will make it in?"

"Surprise. I am here. Arrived late last night. Mom had my bed already turned back, ready for me to crawl in."

"Your mom spoils you," Liz said with a laugh. "Guess your mom has already filled you in on the changes for the Fourth."

"Yes, she did, over breakfast. I think it's a great idea. Having the Fourth at the park is perfect. By the way, can I park the car at your place?" Millie asked.

"Sure, but park around back where the workers park. So, you drove in?" Liz asked.

"No, I flew in this time. Mom has loaned me her car while I'm here. What do your guests think about the Fourth?"

"Oh, Millie, they are so excited. That's why we are having the cookout at the park. Gill came up with the idea and presented it before the church. With the park only a few blocks away, we can prepare the food, then bring some here to the house for our ladies. When it's time for the fireworks, the men at the church fixed a place up on the roof so the ladies can sit up there and watch the display. This way they can enjoy the day and not feel excluded. Just another way to love on them and make them feel important."

"Liz, I think this is wonderful and having them sit up on the roof where no one can see them so they can enjoy the Fourth also."

"Yes, they need this. So, what time are you coming over?"

"I'm almost ready now, say in about twenty to thirty minutes. I want to help Mom and Aunt Dana load the cars up. They have baked and fixed enough for an army, so I can only imagine what the other ladies at the church are bringing. Dad said the men were grilling the burgers and hot dogs."

"I'm sure there will be a good turnout. I saw the sign-up sheet at church, I didn't count, but I'm guessing close to two-hundred people. Some were in charge of the games, decorations and, of course, fireworks. I had the ladies here do some baking for the cake walk. They enjoyed it so much, and I was so pleased at what good cooks we have staying here."

"Liz, your place is so much like a home. I know those ladies must be so grateful."

"At first, they wanted to stay only in the room assigned them, but once we break through the wall they have built, then they begin to come around. The workers we have here are wonderful. Everyone here has a heart for abused women and it shows. The best part is all the workers are volunteers. They have no training for this, yet God led them here with such a giving heart. Even when all our rooms are full or we have a women come in with a child or children, someone shows up to help, and they are perfect for the position needed. Can't tell you how many times I have stopped to pray and thank God for handling all this."

"Have you talked to Glenda lately?" Millie asked?

"Yes, just the other day. She told me you had stopped by, and she told me about Mr. and Mrs. Toppins taking care of her House of Blessings. I think it's wonderful. Maybe someday I will find someone to take over this place, but for now, I think I am where God wants me."

"Liz, don't mean to rush off, but I need to go help load up the cars. I'll see you in a few."

When Liz hung up the phone, she realized Millie never mentioned Scott or Steve. Apparently, she had come by herself. Part of her was glad and another part a little disappointed. Deep down inside, she had to admit, she liked Steve. If only he was local and not so far away.

"Earth to Liz. Can you hear me?" Jana asked.

Looking up, Liz realized Jana must have been talking to her.

"Did you say something, Jana?"

"Liz, I don't know where your mind is, but it's certainly not here. Any more news on Joanna?"

"No, nothing today."

"Wouldn't happen to have your mind on a guy, would you?"

"Jana, you know I haven't been on a date in a very long time."

"You should find someone to date, Liz. You would make some guy a very good catch."

"When the time is right, but for now I'm content with the way things are. Did you need to see me about something, Jana?"

"Oh yes, almost forgot what I came in here to tell you. We have eight cakes, five pies, and two containers of cookies for the cakewalk today. The ladies here have done an excellent job and I feel letting them do this has raised their spirits. You should have seen them. Baking and chatting away, like they were all old friends. Maybe we need to incorporate something like this, and even start a quilt for those that like to sew."

"Jana, that is an excellent idea. I'm sure some ladies from the church would be more than happy to show our ladies here how to quilt or make different dishes. We have always prepared food for them and did the laundry. We haven't really given them something to do. We have Bible study, but they need more. I think some changes are needed here."

"Better run, thought you would like to know what the Masters house is donating for the party today."

"Thanks, Jana."

Gathering up a few things, Liz headed out the back door. As she was crossing the parking lot, she saw Millie pull in. She also noticed; it was only Millie in the car. Deep down inside, she couldn't help but wish the guys had come with her. It would have been nice to spend the Fourth with them, but she needed to brush that thought from her mind. Steve and Scott lived in North Carolina, and she lived in Tennessee. Liz stopped and waited for Millie.

"Hey, Liz perfect timing. Here, let me help you carry some things."

"Thanks, Millie. I'm sure our parents have picked out a spot for us to sit."

"Oh, yes. Our dads were up early this morning with both trucks loaded and headed out to the church to help with other supplies. I think it is so neat the way our parents carry on. Sometimes I don't think they will ever grow up," replied Millie.

Liz laughed. "Would you want them any other way!"

"You're right. Our dads especially. They will always be kids at heart."

As they neared the park, they saw it was beginning to fill up. Tents and tables were set up all around. Finally, they spotted their moms.

Walking over, Millie asked, "Anything we can do to help?"

Looking up, Dana said, "No, girls I think we have got everything here under way. In about thirty- minutes, Pastor Rod will be saying the blessing over the P.A. system. Be sure to listen when they make announcements, that way you will know when the cakewalk and other games will be playing."

Liz spoke up. "I don't think I'll enter the cakewalk. The ladies at the house have shown us they can bake, and I have a feeling there will be a lot of sweets being made from now on."

"Liz, if you win, you could always donate your winnings. Nothing says you have to eat it," Debbie said with a smile.

"You are so right, Aunt Debbie. I never thought about that. Thanks. Now that this is settled, I probably won't win," laughed Liz.

The girls took off to gather up plates of food to take back to the ladies at the Master's house. It was a shame the ladies felt afraid to come and mingle with others, but with all they had been through, they were happy to be able to contribute to the day and be able to see the fireworks that night. As they were gathering things, Liz heard a familiar voice say, "Here, let me carry that. It's way too heavy for you."

When Liz looked up, there was Steve.

"Steve, what are you doing here?" she asked.

"Millie invited Scott and me. We didn't have any plans, so we flew in with her."

"You and Scott are both here and flew in when Millie did? She didn't mention anything about you guys when I spoke to her this morning or when she came over to the house."

"Her dad picked us up at the airport and we stayed with your parents. This morning early, we left with your dads to come help finalize setting up and to help with the cooking. It's been great, so nice to be outside in the fresh air.

Liz wondered why Millie never mentioned to her that Scott and Steve had flown in with her. Why the secret?

"Liz, is it okay if I help you? You seem taken back by seeing me."

"No, no, Steve, I am so sorry. I wasn't expecting to see you and it took me by surprise. Yes, I would appreciate the help. Thanks."

Gathering up the other to-go-boxes, Liz was sure Millie had something up her sleeve. Steve had mentioned Scott was there also, yet she hadn't seen him. Come to think of it, Millie was nowhere in sight, either. Yes, Millie was definitely up to something.

The ladies were so excited when Liz and Steve brought the food in. The smiles on their faces said it all. She was glad Gill had asked the church to have the Fourth celebration at the park. He had said that everyone needs a little happiness in their life, especially these abused women.

On the way back to the park, Liz asked Steve, "So where is Scott? I haven't seen him."

"The last time I saw him, he was helping your pastor unload some things. Pastor Dotson is a really nice guy. When we arrived at the church this morning, after everything was loaded up, he had prayer. I was really touched by what he said. He reminds me of a preacher that comes to our hospital. Mr. Felty can pray such a moving prayer. It's like he is having a conversation with God and God is answering him. Your Pastor Dotson is so much like that."

"Do you know Neal Felty?" Liz asked.

"Yes, I do. In fact, I would say every doctor and nurse at the hospital knows Neal Felty. How do you know him?"

"His daughter, Glenda, is one of my best friends. We went to law school together and were roommates in college. She is the reason I have my home for abused women."

"What a small world," replied Steve. "The Felty family is a very respected family. Mr. Felty keeps hours about like a doctor. He stays on call. By the way, have you ever eaten any of his wife's cooking?"

"I take it you have?" replied Liz.

"Yes, and let me say, that lady can cook. Mr. Felty invited some of us over to his house one weekend. Mrs. Felty was in the kitchen when we arrived. In a short time, she came and said dinner was ready. Let me say, every bite you put in your mouth was sinfully good. I didn't, but I could have licked my plate clean."

"I'm so glad you were able to refrain yourself. It would not have been a good thing for word to get out that Dr. Steve Hunter licked his plate clean after a meal."

"Go ahead and laugh. But if you ever get a chance to eat anything that woman cooks, I promise you it will be awesome." was his reply.

"I'll have to be honest with you. I have had her food, and she is a very good cook."

Steve looked at Liz. "When did you ever eat at her table?"

"Like I said earlier, their daughter Glenda and I are very good friends. I have been to their home and have shared many meals with them. Doris Felty is always cooking for someone. They are a very loving and giving family."

"Absolutely. Like I said, they are well known and respected in Raleigh. In fact, I would say anytime you mention their name anywhere in North Carolina, people know them. I had the privilege of sitting down and talking to Mr. Felty, one on one. He talked to me like I was his son. Offered some good advice and I haven't forgotten. I think of his words often. He really made an impact on me."

"He gave me some words of wisdom once, which I, too, think of often. God has blessed him in a very special way, and he uses that blessing. He and his wife enjoy doing God's work and it shows in so many ways. When they surrendered to the call to serve God, they surrendered all. What a wonderful example they are to everyone." Liz took a deep breath, fighting back a tear.

"Are you alright, Liz?" Steve asked.

"Yes, just thinking about them and how they helped me at a difficult time in my life. I'll never forget it, yet so thankful for how they helped."

Steve reached over and gave Liz a hug. "That's what Christians do. They help others when they need it."

Letting Steve comfort her, Liz realized how his arms around her made her feel so much better. She pulled back, "Thank you. I didn't mean to let my emotions show. I usually have better control than this."

"No worries. Glad I was here," was all Steve said.

Thirteen

$\mathcal{S}$oon it was time for some games. Millie and Scott made several attempts at the cakewalk and finally Scott won. He received a box of homemade cookies. Inside were four different kinds and a dozen of each. Looking at his prize, he said, "I was going to donate my prize, but now that I see what I have won, these may go back on the plane with me."

Steve smiled. "If they make it that long."

"Maybe you need to try your luck at the cakewalk. That way you would have your own snack for the plane!" replied Scott.

"What's this? My brother doesn't want to share. It's not like you to be greedy."

"Steve, I'm going to be like the little red hen. While I was over there going round and round in circles, you were over here sitting and watching. Now, if you had participated and won nothing, that would be different. If you hurry, I do believe you may have time to win you a little something."

Steve looked at Liz. "Let's go. Maybe both of us will win."

Laughing, Steve took Liz by the hand, and they got in the circle for the cakewalk. After a while, they tried the sack race, bottle rings, and balloon popping till they decided they had had enough. On their way back to the canopy where Liz's parents had set up, they passed the cakewalk again. It was still going, and Steve wanted to try again. So, they got in line and when the music stopped and they called out a number, Steve was standing on the number.

"That's me! I finally won."

Turning to Liz, he grabbed her up and swung her around. "Let's go pick out something good." he said.

"No," Liz replied. "You go pick out what you want, I'm going to try to win something. Have you seen that table of goodies? Every time it goes down a little, they fill it back up. Besides, I plan to donate my winnings."

While Steve was trying to decide on what to choose, Liz came up to him.

"Guess what! They stopped on my number. Now let's see what I want."

Liz picked out a container of homemade brownies. Steve chose a red velvet cake.

"So, what charity will we give these to?" he asked.

Looking at her watch, Liz said. "The hospital is not far from here. There is a family in our church that has had so much sickness. The mom has not been able to go home to do anything. Let's fix some to-go boxes and take them our winnings."

"Sounds perfect," Steve said with a smile.

They gathered up the food and headed for the hospital. In the waiting room were Peggy, and three of her children. Kyle, her husband was in surgery. When Liz and Steve walked in with the food, Peggy broke down and cried.

"You will never know how much this means to us. Kyle had to have emergency surgery and I didn't want to bother the pastor for I knew it was the Fourth and he would be at the picnic. God is looking over us and providing."

Liz knelt and took Peggy by the hand. "Would you mind if we prayed with you?"

"Oh, that would be wonderful. We can never have too many prayers," Peggy replied.

"Father, we come to You, asking that You be with Kyle, for he is undergoing surgery. We ask, Father, that You be with everyone performing and assisting in the surgery. Lead their hands with grace and mercy. We know You have the gift to comfort and heal. Father, You are the one who knows all things, sees all things, and can do all things. Fill this family's heart with faith in times of weakness. Thank You for listening to our prayers as we lift this family up to You. Amen."

Peggy, hugged Liz. "I know God sent you. Thank you so much."

"I'll let Rod know and as soon as he can, he will come up and check on you. If you need anything in the meantime, don't hesitate to call. We are always here for you," Liz said as she gave Peggy one more hug.

As they were leaving the hospital Steve asked. "Liz, why did you pick this family to bring food to?"

"While I was walking around at the cakewalk, God placed them in my mind and on my heart. I felt this was what I needed to do, and I am so glad we did what we did."

"Liz, you are a very special lady. Millie speaks very highly of you, and I can understand why. She also says you are an outstanding attorney."

"Steve, don't believe everything Millie says."

"It must be true, for Scott said you helped one of his friends and he was very impressed. He says if he ever needed a lawyer, you would be his first choice. As I understand it, you have never lost a case. Is that right?"

"I don't want to jinx myself, but to date, I have won all my cases. I credit it too much prayer and faith in my heavenly Father. I look to God in all that I do."

"That's why you're so special, Liz."

"How about you? In your line of work, do you rely on God, or your knowledge?"

"Liz, being a doctor, you must rely on God. I pray over every case and several times during it. I'm working on a case now that I have spent much time in prayer over. Studying under this professor and this case has been a blessing for me. Not only am I learning about the human body, but I'm learning what God can do. We as doctors can do so much, but God can do it all. Like you said in your prayer upstairs, God sees all, knows all and can do all things."

As they returned to Liz's car, Chief Helton walked up. "Liz, are you okay?"

"Yes, I'm fine."

"Sorry, but when we noticed you left the park and went to the hospital, we became concerned. No one knew why you left. Just checking to make sure. Your monitor didn't send off any distress signs, but I thought it wise to check on you anyway."

"No, Chief, I'm fine. Appreciate you checking on me. You should have called. I could have saved you a trip."

"You know me, Liz. Just trying to keep you safe. Enjoy the rest of the Fourth."

"You too, Chief."

Steve turned to Liz. "Are you wearing a monitor?"

"Yes, I am. But everything is fine."

"May I ask why?"

"No, it has to do with work, and like you, there are some things you can't discuss."

"Okay, but this does concerns me. I hope you are not in any danger."

"I'm fine. Now, let's get back to the park and see if we can find Millie and Scott."

By the time they made it back to where the family was, Scott was eating a hamburger.

"Scott, are you eating again? How many hamburgers have you had today?" Steve asked.

"For the record, my dear brother, I have had two hamburgers, two hotdogs, three plates of slaw and beans, potato salad, I think two bags of chips, a bag of cotton candy, a bag of kettle corn and I have lost track of the desserts I have consumed. This beats hospital food anytime, and I am enjoying."

"Can't fault you there. Hey, I finally won on the cakewalk. Won a red velvet cake. Liz and I donated it to a family at the hospital."

"Oh, that reminds me, I also ate some of those cookies I won. They are so good." Scott smiled widely.

"Scott, how is your stomach? I have never known you to eat like this!"

"Surprisingly, it's hanging in there. Now tonight might be a different story. You might have to sit up with me if I get a stomachache." Scott peered over his hamburger at Steve.

"Brother, you are a grown man and a doctor. Unless you need surgery, moan quietly," was Steve's reply.

Scott looked at Steve. "Thanks brother, I'll remember that."

Liz spotted Rod Dotson walking across the park. She ran over to him to inform him of Kyle being in surgery, and that Peggy and the children were at the hospital also. He was so appreciative of her letting him know and he said he would follow up on them.

Soon it was time for the fireworks. Liz, Millie, Scott, and Steve were busy helping the ladies up to the roof of the Master house. Gill and several men from the church had already placed chairs for them to sit in. The women were so excited. At nine-thirty the fireworks began. The display lasted about thirty-five minutes. When it was over, and all the ladies were helped back downstairs. Millie, Scott, and Steve headed back to the park to help clean up. Liz stayed behind to make sure everyone at the home was going to be alright. Liz had told the other workers who had stayed with the ladies that afternoon that they could go on and she would stay with them.

After the house became quiet, Liz sat down and reminisced about the day. She thought of Steve grabbing her up and swinging her around when he won at the cakewalk and also when he gave her a hug during their talk. He was so easy to talk to and be around. You couldn't help but like him and Scott. Taking a deep breath, closing her eyes, Liz prayed. Only God knew her heart and how she felt.

Fourteen

The next morning, Millie called early. "Hey, Liz, any plans for the morning?"

"Believe it or not, I have to be in court at ten thirty. Tried every way to get it scheduled for a different time but couldn't swing it. As soon as I'm out, I'll give you a call."

"That is probably not going to work, Liz. We have a flight out at twelve thirty."

"Oh, no. I thought you were going to be home for a few days."

"Like you, our schedules didn't cooperate with our plans. Also, Steve got a call about a patient of his and he is anxious to get back. Liz why don't you plan a trip to Raleigh? You could stay with me. You need a break. Why not stay a week?"

"We will see Millie. Right now, I can't go that far away due to work. If you get a chance, stop by before I have to be in court."

"Okay. See you in a few."

Liz realized she would not be able to see Steve before he went back to Raleigh. She didn't even tell him goodbye last night, thinking she would see him today. He had texted her late last night and said they finally had the park put back together and everything taken back to the church. Here she was again, thinking of Steve. She really needed to get a hold of herself, for in all reality, nothing would ever become of them, and she needed to realize this. Why was she acting like some teenager? Gathering up her things, she left for work.

Pulling into the parking garage, Liz noticed a car just like her mom's. Wondering what her mom was doing here, she hurried upstairs. Walking into her office, their stood Steve.

"Good morning. Hope you don't mind me waiting on you here in your office?"

"No, not at all. I was expecting to see my mom," Liz replied.

"She is here. She is getting her car tags renewed, so I rode along with her. I wanted to say goodbye before we left to go back home. Last night it was rather late when we finished putting things away, so I sent you a text."

"Yes, I received your text and appreciate you letting me know. The ladies at the home really enjoyed yesterday and I want to thank you for all your help."

"Liz, I enjoyed yesterday also, and spending the day with you made the Fourth so much more enjoyable. I know we talk some on the phone, but I want you to know my feelings for you are more than a good friend. I deeply care for you. With us being in two different states and we both have demanding jobs, I'm not how sure this will work out, but for my part, I would like to see if we could work something out. I need to know what your feelings are."

Liz was speechless. So many things going through her mind.

"Liz, do you have anything to say? Have I overstepped my bounds?" Steve asked.

"No, I'm sorry. I wasn't expecting to see you here this morning and I wasn't expecting to hear this."

"I'm sorry, Liz. I thought maybe you felt the same as I do. We get along so well; we like the same things. I don't know, it seems like we hit it off. I apologize for assuming that something was there and putting you on a spot. Please forgive me. Can we still be friends?"

Liz was stilling struggle for the right words to say when Steve turned to walk out the door.

"Steve, wait. I'm not good at this and I'm not good at expressing my feelings especially toward a man. If we were in a courtroom, it would be different, I would have all kinds of words to say, but when it comes to my personal life, I clam up. I share very little."

Steve smiled. "That's understandable. So, can you share with me your feelings?"

Taking a deep breathe, Liz dropped her head and thinking to herself, "Dear Lord, please help me. Give me the right words to say. I know what I want to say but I want it to be what You know is best."

Steve stepped over and took Liz's hand. "If you need some time, that's okay. I don't want to pressure you into something you don't want. Pray about. If it's not right, God will let you know."

"Steve, to be honest, I do care about you. I'm worried that with us being so far apart, it won't work. I don't want either one of us to be hurt, due to the distance between us."

"I can understand that. I'm only asking that we try to make it work. If we don't put forth some effort, we will never know. If I didn't care so much for you, I wouldn't be standing here."

Dana walked in the door. "Well, I got those car tags. Are you ready to go back to the house, Steve?"

"Can I meet at your car, Mrs. Barnett?"

Dana realize she had walked in at the worst time possible. Walking over to Liz, she gave her a hug and kiss on the cheek. Turning to go out the door she said, "Take your time Steve, I'll be downstairs. See you, Liz." And out the door she went.

Liz smiled. "Sorry about that."

Laughing, Steve said, "I bet tonight your mom will barrage you with a million questions."

"No, she is good at not questioning me. Now Millie's mom, Debbie, that's a whole other story. She should have been an attorney. Before you can answer her question, she is firing another one."

"So that's how you became an attorney, from your aunt."

"Good point, but she also likes to take care of you. She always said she should have gone into nursing. It's a good thing that she didn't. Can you image being sick, her taking care of you and firing fifty questions at you at once? Not a good thought to have."

"True. Now back to what we were talking about. You know how to reach me. You let me know what you want."

Leaning over, he kissed Liz on the cheek and walked out the door. Still stunned by what had just taken place, Liz wasn't sure what to think or do. She was stilling standing in the same spot when Dee walked in.

"Are you ready for court this morning?" Dee asked.

Liz, still miles away in thought, didn't respond.

"Liz, are you alright?"

Looking sort of startled, Liz replied, "I'm sorry, Dee, did you say something?"

"Did you have a good Fourth? You seem miles away. Is everything okay with Joanna?"

"I'm alright. Need to pull myself together and get this morning going. Now, what is on the agenda for today?" Liz asked.

Dee looked at Liz. "Did you hear me come in and say something to you? You do realize you are at work, and this is court day?"

"Yes, I know what day this is. Do you have the papers?"

"Liz, you took everything home with you, so you could study over them. Are they not in your briefcase?"

"Yes, yes, you are right. It slipped my mind. Okay. Give me a minute and we will be ready."

"This is not like you. What's wrong with you this morning? I'm a little concerned here," replied Dee.

"Don't worry, I'm fine. I just need a few minutes to myself."

"Liz, are you looking for something?"

"Yes, my briefcase. I know I had it here."

Dee walked over to Liz's desk, picked it up and handed it to Liz. "Here it is. Must been hiding from you."

Feeling a little flush and foolish, Liz said, "Thanks, Dee. That will be all for now."

Dee was puzzled as she left Liz's office and closed the door behind her. She had never seen Liz like this before and questioned what was going on with her. If anyone was on top of things, it was Liz. Even with everything about Joanna, Chief

Helton, and wearing a monitor, Liz always had it together. What had her so shaken up like this?

Sitting at her desk, Liz bowed her head and began to pray. Seeing Steve this morning and hearing what he had to say was something she wasn't expecting. Yes, she cared for him and yes, she would like to date him, but how could this possibly work when they lived so far apart? Then several verses of scripture came to her.

Philippians 4:13: *"I can do all things through Christ my Lord who strengthens me."*

Psalm 62:8: *"Trust in him at all times, O people; pour out your hearts to him, for God is our refuge."*

Proverbs 19:21: *"Many are the plans in a man's heart, but it is the Lord's purpose that prevails."*

Yes, she thought. I will give this all to God. He will give me the strength I need. I will trust Him for He is my refuge, He will guide me. It's not what I want, but what God wants. His purpose will prevail. What was it Pastor Rod said the three Ps of faith were: presence, prayer, and patience. With that Liz gathered her things and left for the courtroom. She had a peace come over her and she knew God was working it all out.

It was after twelve when court was dismissed. Liz called Millie.

"Hey, sorry we didn't get together this morning. Maybe we can talk later tonight when we both get home."

"Yeah, I came by your office, but Dee said you had already left for court, and I didn't want to bother you. I'll give you a call tonight and we can chat then. Love you, Liz."

"Love you, too, Millie."

That night Millie called, and they talk for only a few minutes. Not once did Millie mentioned Scott or Steve. As Liz got ready for bed, she wondered if she would hear from Steve or if he was giving her time and waiting for her to make the next move. Until she felt led to call or text him, she would just wait.

Fifteen

It had been three weeks since the Fourth celebration. Liz hadn't heard from Steve or Millie. As she sat at her desk pondering, Dee buzzed her.

"Liz, you have a call from Duke on line two."

"Thanks Dee."

Liz answered the phone, "This is Liz Barnett."

"Yes, Miss Barnett, this is Dr. Tad Reagan. Have you a minute to talk?"

"Yes, I do. How is Joanna?"

"Miss Barnett, do you think it is possible that you could come here to Duke? It is about Miss Joanna. We feel your visit here would be most beneficial. I realize this is a short notice and your schedule is probably very full, but if you could arrange it, I don't think you would regret it."

"Dr. Reagan, has Joanna taken a turn for the worse? I thought she was making progress!"

"Miss Joanna has quite a few things going on with her right now. I wouldn't ask you to come if it wasn't important. The sooner you can come, the better," Dr. Reagan replied.

"Yes, I will check with my secretary and see how my schedule looks. Maybe I can get a flight out within the next day or so, but I can't promise you."

"Miss Barnett, when you have things arranged to leave Nashville, send me a text so we will know when to expect you. Thank you and hope to see you soon. Goodbye."

Liz had so many thoughts going through her mind. Was Joanna dying? Why else would Dr. Reagan call and ask her to come to Duke? Dee walked into Liz's office.

"Is everything okay?" she asked.

"I'm not sure. That was Dr. Tad Reagan and he said I needed to come to Duke as soon as I could. What does my schedule look like, and do you think you could call the airlines to see how soon you can book me a flight?"

"Do you have any idea how many days you will be gone, and do you want a round trip ticket?"

"Tell me about my schedule and we will work from that," Liz said, rubbing her head. So many things were going through her mind.

Liz called her mom and told her what was going on.

"Honey, don't worry about anything. When you get a flight, let us know and one of us will take you to the airport. Also, I will call Pastor Dotson and get the prayer chain going. Joanna is going to be alright. She is in God's hands, and He has brought her a long way."

"I know, I just needed to hear your voice. Here I am a grown woman, needing to hear her mom's voice."

"Liz, you have no idea how many times I would love to hear my mom's voice. It's been fifteen years and I still miss her so much. Some things you never outgrow."

"Thanks Mom. If I haven't told you lately, 'I love you and Dad.' I am so blessed to have wonderful godly parents. I know with my work I don't come around often, but you guys are the very best."

"Liz, we love you and are so proud of you. You have worked hard for what you have become. It's not anything your dad and I did. You have done it all on your own."

"I don't know what's wrong with me. I'm not an emotional person, but after receiving that phone call, it did something to me."

"Liz, take some time to pray. Time alone with God will do you good. In the meantime, I will be praying for you and will make some phone calls. Love you, honey."

"Thanks, Mom. Love you, too."

Dee walked in with Liz's schedule. "Good news. You were scheduled with court tomorrow, but when I checked the emails, it was rescheduled to next Wednesday. You have some appointments, but nothing that I can't reschedule. I will say, you had an unexpected emergency out of town."

Chief Helton came bursting through the door. "Liz, what's going on?"

Looking up at him, Liz replied. "Nothing. What's supposed to be going on?"

"Your monitor is acting up again. I got here as soon as I could. Has someone upset you?" he said.

Realizing what had happened, Liz said, I'm fine, but I'm really glad you are here. I hadn't thought of it till you mentioned it, but I am going to be going out of town and will need to remove the monitor."

"Absolutely not, Liz. That monitor stays on for a while longer and you don't need to be going out of town. Send someone else," was his reply.

"Sorry, Chief, but I am going, and I will be removing the monitor."

"May I ask where you're going and for how long?"

Liz proceeded to explain to Chief Helton about the phone call she had received. He stood looking at her for a few minutes and then smiled.

"I have a solution."

Sergeant Jordan was standing in Dee's office when Chief Helton called him into Liz's office.

"Liz, here is your travel companion. Sergeant Jordan will accompany you wherever you go."

"Chief, I don't need a bodyguard. I will be perfectly fine," Liz said.

Sergeant Jordan spoke up, "Sir, if I may ask, where are you sending me?"

"My young man, Liz here is going to be traveling to Raleigh, North Carolina, and you are going with her. You are to stay by her side and never let her out of your sight."

"Sir, the next few days are my off days. I have already pull extra duty and you had told me I could be off," Sergeant Jordan stated.

"I'm sorry, but you know this case, and I will feel better if you are the one to accompany Liz while she is out of town."

Chief Helton turned to Liz and said, "When you purchase your plane ticket, let me know the cost for Sergeant Jordan, and the department will reimburse you. Do you know how long you will be gone and where you plan to stay?"

Looking at Chief Helton, Liz replied. "You really think this is necessary. I will be staying with my cousin and when I'm not with her, more than likely I will be at the hospital. You are carrying this a little too far. I have been patient and worn the monitor as you asked. Joanna has been at Duke for nearly three months, and we haven't seen or heard from the man we think is her father. The monitor is coming off, I will not put it back on, and I don't need Sergeant Jordan following me around."

"Liz, in North Carolina, we can't protect you. What if the guy knows where she is and that's the reason we haven't heard from him? Let Drew go with you, just to be on the safe side. I will feel so much better. Then when you get back, we will discuss the monitor."

Liz looked around the room. "I'll need to think about this."

Dee spoke up. "Liz, you need to decide soon, for I need to call the airlines and tell them how many seats we need. Trying to get the next flight out and asking for two seats could be difficult."

"Alright, I don't like it, but he can go. But understand Chief, when I return, I will not be wearing that monitor anymore."

Chief Helton patted Liz on the shoulder. "Wise decision, and I will feel much better while you are gone. I will call ahead and get all security clearance for Sergeant Jordan for his flight."

Turning to Sergeant Jordan, Chief Helton said, "Drew, my young man, you are dismissed for the day. Go home and pack, and when the arrangements have been made, Dee here will let you know. You guys have a safe trip." Chief Helton turned and walked out the door.

Liz looked at Sergeant Jordan. "If you don't mind, I will refer to you as Drew. That will keep down stares and people murmuring."

Drew Jordan turned and walked away, shaking his head. He knew Chief Helton relied on him a lot and that he was the Chief's first choice on anything, but he was so looking forward to having the next few days off.

Liz went home to pack, hoping Dee could pull a miracle on getting them a flight out. Her phone rang and sure enough it was Dee.

"Hey girl, did you have any luck?"

"Liz, I was able to get two seats on a flight out to Raleigh. Sorry, but it leaves at three in the morning."

"That's okay. Maybe I can sleep some on the plane."

"Oh, one thing more. The two seats are not together. They are three rows apart. This was the best I could do. I informed Chief Helton that I had booked the flight, but I never mentioned where the seats were. He has all the other information."

"That's alright, Dee. What he doesn't know won't hurt him and besides, I really don't need Drew by my side constantly. This is definitely an overkill. If anything comes up at the office, give me a call and when I get there and find out what all is going on, I'll let you know. Thanks, Dee, for all your help. I don't know what I would do without you."

"Liz, you are most welcome. I pray you will receive good news when you get there. See you when you get back."

Liz called her mom and told her what time she would need to be picked up to go to the airport.

She could have driven and left her car at the airport, but she knew that wouldn't do. Between her parents and Chief Helton, Liz at times felt like a child. Maybe one day, they would realize she was a grown women and not fuss over her so much, but then if they didn't, she would think they didn't care. She was grateful that they cared so much. Then she thought of Joanna, how her parents didn't show her love and compassion. How could a parent not love their child?

When Liz arrived at the airport, she went ahead and checked in. Looking around she saw Drew Jordan was waiting on her.

"What time did you get here, Drew?" Liz asked.

"Oh, Chief Helton had me here early. He had to make sure I made it through security. You just missed him. I went and got a coffee at Starbucks and got you one, too. Hope you like it."

"Thanks. You can't go wrong with Starbucks. I haven't found a drink from there that I haven't liked. That place can be addictive."

When they found the correct terminal, Liz and Drew found a seat and waited on the plane.

Liz asked Drew, "How long have you worked for Chief Helton?"

"Let's see. When I was in high school, I cleaned offices in our building and his was one of them. He took a liking to me and was the one to encourage me to go into law enforcement. That was ten years ago. He has always looked after me, and I don't have the heart to turn him down when he gives me an extra assignment. He is like a dad to me," was Drew's reply.

"Where are your parents, if you don't mind me asking?"

"No, I don't mind. My parents were killed in a boating accident and my grandmother raised me."

"I'm sorry, Drew. I know that has been hard on you."

"I was thirteen when they were killed. My grandmother lived next door to Chief Helton's mother. When he found out about my parents, he would have me come to the station after school, and I would pick up the trash and little things like that. Then as I got older, the cleaning company that cleaned the building hired me. That's how I know so many people in the building."

"So, Chief Helton got you started in the cleaning business also," laughed Liz.

"Yeah, you could say that. He is really a nice guy. When I was young, doing little things like emptying the trash or whatever, at the end of the week he always gave me money. Said I had done a great job and had earned it. To me, it was really something to be thirteen, working at the police station and getting paid. I owe him a lot. Like I said, he is a dad to me."

"Drew, thanks for sharing that with me. I never knew Chief Helton had an understanding side to him. He always comes across to me differently."

"He cares about you and has a lot of respect for you. I don't know of another attorney in the building that he speaks as highly of as he does you. He has your safety in mind."

"I suppose," was all Liz could say.

Finally, their flight number was called. When they boarded the plane, Drew realized the seating.

"Miss Barnett, you sit up here, and I'll take the back seat. This way I will be able to see you."

"Chief Helton has trained you well," Liz said.

Before long, the plane had landed at Raleigh/Durham. Millie was waiting for them.

"Hey, you guys, so glad to see you. Want to grab some breakfast somewhere before we head out to Duke?"

"If it's okay, Millie could we grab something at the snack bar at the hospital?" Liz said.

"Liz, we have a good forty-five-minute drive, depending on traffic, maybe a little longer. They are working on the roads and traffic is bad. So, are you guys hungry?"

Drew spoke up. "You pick the place and I'll buy. I'm starved."

Millie found a chicken and waffle place to eat not far from the airport.

Drew laughed, "Girl you can't go wrong with chicken or waffles for breakfast. Hope you are not in a hurry to get to the hospital, Liz. This may take a while."

When they walked in the restaurant, the smell of food was so good. Drew looked at the menu. "I may have one of everything."

Liz looked at him. "Why don't we pick you up on our way back."

The food was delicious, Liz had to admit, but she also was anxious to get to the hospital. Finally, they were back on the road, and as Millie had predicted, traffic was terrible. It took an hour and ten minutes to arrive at the hospital. Millie took Liz and Drew up to the sixth floor. When the elevator doors open, there was a huge sitting area. Millie had them to wait there while she went to notify the doctors.

Dr. Riley Cameron came out to meet them.

"Miss Barnett, it is so nice to finally meet you. Is this your husband?"

"No, this is a friend who came with me. How is Joanna doing?"

"Miss Barnett, you are going to see a tremendous change in Joanna. Dr. Reagan will be out soon to talk to you. There have been four doctors working on her case. Before he could name the other doctors, Dr. Reagan arrived."

"Miss Barnett, I am Dr. Reagan. If you will have a seat, we will discuss Joanna."

Taking a seat, Liz wanted more than anything to see Joanna, but she also needed to hear what the doctors had to say.

"First of all, our Joanna is fully awake. She is learning to talk, and she is in therapy to relearn how to walk. She knows the people that have been with her for the past few months, but she has no memory of her past. She doesn't remember being hurt but she does remember being in a hospital and remembers a lady that visited her often. Millie had a message from you on her phone, and when we played it for Joanna, she recognized your voice."

Liz could feel tears forming in her eyes. Joanna remembered her. What a blessing.

"Miss Barnett, when you walk in, until you speak, she will not know you. Millie purchased some clothes for her, and they are getting her dressed as we speak. I know this is going to be very emotional for you, for you have a bond with that young girl, and she remembers your kindness."

As Liz tried hard to pull herself together, Drew reached over and patted her on the back.

"You going to be, okay?" he asked.

Nodding her head that she would, Liz took a deep breath. She had waited so long for this day, and now it was here. She was going to see Joanna without bandages, tubes, and monitors.

Dr. Reagan stood up. "If you're ready, follow me."

They turned to go down a hall and stopped at the first door on the right. Dr. Reagan opened the door and motioned for Liz to go in. When she stepped in the room, sitting in a chair was this beautiful young lady. Liz could not move, she froze. All she could do was look at Joanna.

The young girl smiled and said in a broken voice. "Are you looking for me?"

Through tears, Liz smiled. "Yes, I believe you are the young girl I'm looking for."

When Liz spoke, Joanna smiled and had tears in her eyes. "You are the lady, that helped me. You read to me and prayed. Always telling me I was going to get better. I couldn't talk but you were so encouraging. I wanted so much to say something back, but I couldn't."

Liz walked over to Joanna and knelt to hug her. The two hugged and never said a word. Finally, Liz pulled back. "You are so beautiful. God has answered our prayers."

"You told me over and over that God was with me and would never leave me. You said it so much that I truly believed it, and you were right. You also said God was going to heal me and He has. You are an angel that God sent to me. How can I ever thank you?"

"Joanna, seeing you here today is all the thanks I need. You are a miracle and a special blessing."

Reaching over, Liz gave Joanna another hug.

Dr. Cameron spoke up. "Joanna needs to go for some therapy now. You two can visit more later. Miss Barnett, if you will follow us, we can go somewhere to talk."

Patting Joanna on the cheeks, Liz smiled and said, "I'll be back after your therapy."

Walking down the hall with the doctors, Liz was on cloud nine. Yes, she had to listen closely as Joanna spoke but still, she could talk, make sentences. She was learning to walk and use her arms and legs. This day was perfect. What a blessing it had turned out to be.

Dr. Cameron led her to a room that was like a conference room. As she and Drew sat down, Dr. Cameron asked them if they would like some coffee. Liz noticed Millie was nowhere to be seen. Soon Dr. Reagan walked in.

"We are waiting on two more doctors to come in that have worked very close with Joanna. They, like ourselves, can answer any questions you may have."

Soon Dr. Warren came in. When he spoke, Liz knew she had spoken to him on the phone about Joanna. Then Steve Hunter walked in. Liz looked at him, not knowing what to say.

"Miss Barnett, this is Dr. Steve Hunter. He works very closely under Dr Warren. He is a fine young doctor, and we feel very fortunate to have him."

Liz didn't know what to say. Steve had said he was working on a very unusual case, but she had no idea it was Joanna. All she could do was look down at her hands. What was she to say?

Dr. Warren spoke by saying, "Our Joanna has been a very challenging case. When she came to us from Nashville, I was afraid we would not be able to help her. We studied her case over and over and Dr. Hunter here found the answer we were looking for. We credit her recovery to him. We all worked with her, but Dr. Hunter is the one who really saved her life. Miss Barnett, we realize you were very close to the young girl. Do you have any questions for us?"

So many things were going through Liz's mind. Where would she start? Finally, she asked, "Why don't you tell me her prognosis? Will she be able to be a normal, healthy young girl? Will she suffer from any of her injuries?"

Steve spoke up. "Joanna will probably have arthritis set in from all her broken bones as time goes on. We don't have any family history on her, so some things we can only guess at. From what I have learned from people I've interviewed who have PTSD from trauma such as rape, they had nightmares and irrational fears until the memory of the trauma resurfaced with therapy and could be dealt with. The mind retains even if it isn't on a conscious level. Until her memory completely returns, the chances of her having nightmares, fear of certain things or people is very unlikely."

Liz asked. "Does she seem strong?"

Dr. Warren spoke up. "She is making remarkable progress. It will take some time for her strength to get where it should be, but if she keeps going the way she has, she should do just fine."

"How is her vision? When she was left at my doorstep, her face and eyes were so swollen?"

"We have tested her vision, and it is twenty/twenty," replied Dr. Cameron.

"Miss Barnett, Joanna has gone through so many operations. Being young and a fighter has helped her a lot. Also, all the encouraging words from you during such a critical time in her life. A lady named Gloria Felty comes by and reads to Joanna. They have prayer. Joanna told her of her special friend that always read and prayed for her. That friend was you," said Dr. Reagan.

"That child didn't deserve to be treated the way she was. I'm so thankful she was left at my doorstep. Also, I'm so thankful she has had Gloria Felty here by her side. I know that family and they are very special."

"Miss Barnett, if you have no further questions for us, we are going to go on about our day. If you think of anything, we will see you tomorrow, I'm sure, and you can ask us then," Dr. Warren said.

Liz and Drew remained seated as the doctors left. Then Steve walked back into the room.

Looking at Drew, he said. "Liz, may we talk, privately?"

Drew stood up to walk out but turned to Liz. "I'll be right outside the door."

Steve took a seat by Liz. "I know seeing me this morning was a shock to you. I didn't know till two days ago that you were the one Joanna kept talking about. I was having dinner with Scott and Millie the other night when I asked Millie if by any chance she would have known Joanna since she had come from Nashville. She filled me in on the story and said that you were the one who gave her the name Joanna. That then explained why you were wearing a monitor. I asked Millie if she had your voice on a message on her phone. She did. I borrowed it, and when Joanna heard your voice, she stated that you were her friend. That's why you were contacted to come here."

"Why didn't Millie tell me? When I called her to see if I could stay with her, she never said a word."

"Liz, I asked Millie not to say anything. I knew you would ask a lot of questions, and she hasn't worked on this case and would not have been able to answer you."

"Steve, the other doctors called to give me updates on her. Why did you never call?"

"I'm studying under Dr. Warren. I studied Joanna's case, treated her, and that's all. When the other doctors made a remark that they would contact her friend to give her an update, they never mentioned your name. When they discussed what to tell you, I was not included in that conversation. I never knew who called you. All of this came to light two days ago. Liz, I never meant to keep anything about her case from you intentionally."

"I was so surprised when you walked in. So many things are going through my mind. I need some time to think."

"Liz, write your questions down. We will be happy to answer them. I'll go see if Joanna is finished with therapy, so you two can visit again."

Steve had stepped into the hall when Dr. Cameron came walking up.

"Steve, is Miss Barnett still here?"

"Yes, I was on my way to see if Joanna was finished with therapy so the two could visit again."

Dr. Cameron smiled. "Good, I have someone I want her to meet." Turning to the woman that was with him, he said, "I want you to meet the lady that helped Joanna so much."

They walked into the conference room where Liz and Drew sat.

"Miss Barnett, I have someone I want you to meet," Dr. Cameron said. "This is Beth McCloud. Mrs. McCloud, Liz Barnett."

Mrs. McCloud walked over to Liz to shake her hand. "It is a pleasure to meet you. I was so excited when I heard you were coming. I want you to know we are going to take excellent care of Joanna, and you are more than welcome to come visit her anytime you can."

Looking a little baffled, Liz was not sure what the lady was talking about. Finally, Liz said, "Are you a nurse or a doctor?"

Dr. Cameron spoke up. "Miss Barnett, Mrs. McCloud is going to adopt Joanna. They have been looking for some time for a child to adopt, and when they heard about Joanna, they came to see her and fell in love with her."

Looking shocked, Liz replied, "That's wonderful. Joanna needs a good home, but I wasn't expecting it to be so soon."

"Well, she has made remarkable progress, and when Mr. and Mrs. McCloud came to visit with her, they talked to Joanna, and it was like the child progressed even more. I believe they were meant to be together," Dr. Cameron said.

"Miss. Barnett, when I first saw Joanna, it is really hard to explain, but it was like I already knew her. There was something that drew her so close to me. I knew right then, that she was to go home with us. We have three sons, two are grown, one is still in college. We had been praying about adopting a child, and I had shared this with a friend of ours who happens to know Pastor Felty. They spoke to him, for he is around so many people, and he then shared with them some information about Joanna. They told us, so then we called Pastor Felty. Arrangements were made for us to visit the girl and we fell in love with her. We knew right away this was what God wanted for us. We have already been fixing up a room for her in our home. Having had all boys, I am so thrilled to be having a daughter."

Liz smiled. "God does have a way of working things out for the best. Do you live here in Raleigh?"

"Oh, no. We live in Lexington, Kentucky."

"That's closer to Nashville than Raleigh is," Liz said.

"That's right. You are more than welcome to come visit Joanna anytime. If I may ask, what all do you know about Joanna?"

"To be honest, I don't know very much. She was left at my doorstep in very bad shape. We didn't know her name and she was in no condition to tell us, so I gave her the name Joanna, for it means 'God is gracious.' We know of a man that said his daughter was a runaway and we think maybe our Joanna was who he was looking for. So, for her protection, it was decided to send her here to Raleigh, which has proven to be a blessing in many ways."

"Oh, Miss Barnett, I totally agree."

"Please call me Liz."

"If you will call me Beth. So, for a last name, what should she go by for now?"

"I have a dear friend that is an attorney here in Raleigh, in fact she is Pastor Neal Felty's daughter. I will give her a call and I'm sure she can help you with all that."

"Someone told me you were an attorney. Can you not take care of this for us?"

"Yes, but I will be going home tomorrow. Glenda is an outstanding attorney, and she can make things happen. Also, she is not as attached to Joanna as I am, and I think it would be better all-around if she handled things."

"I understand. I'm sorry, I wasn't thinking this through."

"Trust me. Beth, I'll be in touch with Glenda. Also, you have Neal and Doris Felty praying about this. They are the best prayer warriors you will ever find. I do believe they have a special connection with our Heavenly Father."

"I'm inclined to agree with you, Liz. The first time my husband and I met them, they just gathered us in. You could feel the love they had to offer, and they do this to everyone. If we lived here, I would attend his church, for I know his congregation must feel so blessed. Another question, if you don't mind. If the man you spoke of is Joanna's dad, do you think he would come looking for her?"

"I really don't think so. You see, we never told him the name we gave her. He has no idea if his daughter is alive or dead. Unless, by some small chance, he happens to be in Lexington and recognizes her, I don't think you have anything to worry about. He doesn't know she was sent here to Raleigh. For all he knows, she is still in Nashville."

"That's good to know. Did Joanna tell you that she would like to go to college and go into medicine? She is so grateful for what the doctors have done for her, she wants to someday be able to help others. We told her she could study in whatever field she wanted. She has our full support."

"Beth, this blesses me so much. That girl deserves a good home and I believe God has led her to just that. When they first said she was going to be adopted, I was a little taken back, but now, I am so happy for her. I'm so grateful that I came to see her and that I have had the privilege to meet you."

"I'm glad you came too, for I wanted to meet the lady that was so instrumental in her recovery and encouraged her not to give up. You will always be very special to her Liz."

Sixteen

That night, back at Millie's apartment, Liz, Drew, and Millie sat around talking and decided to order pizza for dinner. Liz shared with Millie about the adoption for Joanna. Millie had no idea and was so excited. Liz also found out that Millie had no idea that Steve was working on Joanna's case. Feeling tired, they decided to turn in. Millie turned to Drew.

"I never thought to ask, but do you have a place to stay tonight?"

"I have to stay where Liz stays," was his reply.

"I only have a one-bedroom apartment. Liz can share my bed but all I have to offer you is the floor or this loveseat and it's only big enough for two people to sit on. How tall are you by the way?"

Laughing Drew said, "I'm six-two."

"Oh. Your legs will probably hang off unless you curl up in a fetal position all night."

"The loveseat will do fine. Sorry to be an inconvenience to you, but Chief's orders are that I stay close by Liz."

Millie shook her head. "It's no inconvenience for me, but not sure how you will feel in the morning. I'll bring you a pillow and some blankets."

When Liz and Millie had gone to bed, Millie started laughing. "Drew is going to feel really rough in the morning! I bet before the night is over, he ends up on the floor."

"He didn't need to come, but Chief Helton has it in his head that I still need protection. Drew is a really nice guy. By the way Millie, he is single, and you will have to admit he is rather cute."

"Thanks, Liz, but I have my eye on Scott, and I think he feels the same about me. How are things with you and Steve?"

"We haven't really had a chance to talk. At first, I was mad at him for not saying anything to me about Joanna, but then when I thought about it, I realized that I had never mentioned her to him. He does seem like an excellent doctor, and the other doctors speak very highly of him."

"Scott told me that to do what Steve does, takes a special person. He said Steve's knowledge on medicine and the human body surpasses him. Don't get me wrong, Scott is very knowledgeable but he has had to study harder, as for Steve, medical school was no struggle to him. His mind retains all that he reads and studies. That's why he was accepted to study under Dr. Warren. They were all impressed with how well Steve could do."

"That's why God made all of us so different. Take me, I could not do what you do, Millie, and I'm sure studying law is something you would not want to do. We have to find out what our purpose here is and make the very best of it. Joanna, I know in my heart, will do wonderfully. I'm so excited to see what God has in store for her."

"Liz, is that Drew snoring?"

"Sounds like it. He is making good use of your loveseat after all." Laughing, the two turned over and went to sleep.

The next morning, Liz went to the kitchen to put on a pot of coffee. She sniggered to herself when she saw Drew. He was lying on his stomach with one arm and leg hanging off the front of the love seat, the other leg over the arm, and his back looked bowed. She thought to herself, you are going to have a hard time getting up and when you do, you will feel rough.

Millie came walking in and when she saw Drew she said, "Oh my. That poor guy is going to be miserable when he gets up. Should we go ahead and wake him?"

"When we start moving around in the kitchen, he will probably wake up. Millie, do you use regular or decaf coffee?"

"Oh, regular. Working at the hospital, you need the strong stuff."

Drew was beginning to move. They could hear him moan and grunt. Finally, he fell into the floor. Slowly, he stood up and when he turned, there stood Millie and Liz in the kitchen.

Liz asked, "How did you sleep last night?"

Millie said, "What's important, how do you feel?"

"To answer both questions, I slept okay, tossed and turned quite a bit. How do I feel? I have pain most all over my body. If we stay here tonight, I'll make a bed on the floor, thank you. Now, if you ladies don't mind, I'm going to take a hot shower and see if I can't loosen up my body."

Turning to go take a shower, Millie and Liz laughed when Drew was out of earshot. Millie leaned close to Liz, "Poor guy, he walked like he was in pain."

Later that morning, Liz went back to the hospital to tell Joanna goodbye. When Joanna left Nashville, Liz had prayed over her, hugged her the best she could. This time, Joanna stood up, wrapped her arms around Liz, gave her a big hug, and kissed her on the cheek.

"I'll always be grateful to you. I know others prayed over me when I was in a coma, but your prayers I remember the most. Your tender, loving voice telling me over and over I was going to get better, and that God was always with me. I believe He was, because there were times I felt like someone was holding me in their arms. It was so comforting. I never knew much about God until you came into my life. You were so faithful in your visits. When I came out of the coma and was able to talk so they could understand me, I asked Pastor Felty and his wife about this man named God. I told him a lady I didn't know her name came by my bed every day. She prayed and talked about how loving and caring God was. I asked him how I could meet this man. He and his wife shared the most beautiful story of Jesus. They made arrangements that day to take me down to the chapel here in the hospital. There, Pastor Felty baptized me. You started me down that path and Pastor Felty led me the rest of the way. This is why you will always hold a special place in my heart."

The two hugged and both had tears rolling down their cheeks. God's presence could certainly be felt.

"Joanna, I will always be available if you ever need me. If you want to just talk, I am here for you. You hold a very special place in my heart, and I love you so much. Knowing you have let Christ into your life is an even greater blessing."

The therapist came to the door and said, "Hate to interrupt, but it's time for your therapy."

"I have a plane to catch later this afternoon, so I'll go ahead and say goodbye. Promise me, to stay in touch. I gave Beth McCloud my card so she has my number. Call me anytime you want. I love you, Joanna, and I'm so proud of you."

They both hugged and cried, then the therapist led Joanna out of the room. Liz walked to the door to watch Joanna walk down the hall, a sight she had prayed to see.

Joanna turned to look back at Liz. "You are my angel and always will be." Then she continued to therapy.

Liz and Drew walked over to the elevator and when the door opened, Steve was standing there.

"Liz, I'm so glad to see you. Can we go somewhere to talk?"

Looking at Drew, "Can you go get yourself some coffee or a snack? Tell me where you'll be and when we are finished, I'll find you."

"Liz, you know I'm not to let you out of my sight."

"I'm with a friend, Drew, I will be alright."

Steve spoke up. "I promise to take good care of her, and I will personally deliver her to you."

Nodding his head, Drew said, "I will be in the cafeteria when you're finished," then walked to the elevator.

"You have yourself a pretty good bodyguard. How long does he have to keep following you around?"

"When I get back to Nashville, I plan to get my life back. I don't think the person that they thought was following me is anymore."

"So why do they think someone was following you? Is this why you were wearing a monitor on the Fourth?" Steve asked with a concerned look on his face.

"This all had to do with Joanna. I haven't felt like I am being followed in a good while. Chief Helton thinks otherwise."

"So, this explains why on the Fourth he sought you out," Steve said. "In fact, as I think back, this explains a lot of things. How do you feel about Joanna being adopted and moving to Kentucky?"

"Actually, I'm okay with it. Lexington, Kentucky, is much closer to me should I want to go visit her and too, after speaking with Beth McCloud, I had a peace come over me. I feel this is where Joanna belongs. God has worked this all out perfectly."

"With my patient doing so well and leaving, I am going to have a little free time till my next patient in a coma comes in. Think it possible we could spend some time together?" Steve asked.

"Are you planning a trip to Nashville, because my plane leaves this afternoon? I'm to be in court tomorrow, and Dee has already rearranged my schedule so I could come here."

"I was hoping you were going to be staying a few days here. Anyway, you could come back, say in a week?"

Liz looked at Steve's face. His eyes seemed to be pleading with her.

"When I get back home, I'll look my schedule over. At the moment I can't make any promises."

Steve placed his hands on both sides of Liz's shoulders. "You know, if I didn't care for you, I wouldn't be asking. I know Millie would let you stay with her."

Liz could feel her heart beating ever so fast. She was so thankful she didn't have the monitor on.

"Am I overstepping my bounds here?" Steve asked.

Taking a deep breath, Liz said, "No, you're not. I wish so much you lived in Nashville. We have really good hospitals and I'm sure they would be thrilled to have an outstanding doctor like you in their midst."

"So, if I worked in Nashville, things would be better between us, is that what you are saying?"

"I think it would make it easier. With you being in one state while I'm in another only complicates things."

"Why do you feel like that, Liz? If we truly care for each other, it can work. Where is your faith?"

"My faith has nothing to do with this. Do you have any idea how many divorces there are because of spouses not being together?"

"I'm sorry. I didn't realize we were talking marriage. You are ahead of me on this."

"I'm not talking about us getting married, I'm saying when you put distance between a couple, it puts a strain on things. I don't want you to meet someone here and feel you have an obligation to me or vice versa."

"Are you seeing someone in Nashville?" Steve asked.

"No. I haven't dated in long time."

"So, you don't have an obligation to anyone in Nashville, am I understanding you correctly?"

"Steve, you are making this very difficult. You are not understanding what I'm saying."

"Oh, I understand perfectly. What you are telling me, I have my work cut out for me, but don't worry, once I set my mind to something, I make it happen. Wait and see."

"Well, I will let you know, that when I set my mind on something I see it through also. That's why I have such a good reputation as an attorney. Ask your brother, for he himself once told me if he ever needed an attorney, I was number one on his list."

"My brother has spoken about you, but what he said will stay between him and me."

"Are you saying he spoke in a negative way about me?" Liz asked with raised eyebrows.

"Like I said, what my brother and I discussed will stay between us. Guess we had better go find your bodyguard or he may come looking for you. Hate for him to accuse me of kidnapping you."

Liz realized Steve was picking at her. Deep down, she really didn't mind, for she knew he really cared about her, and in a way, she cared about him.

When Liz and Steve walked into the cafeteria, Drew was having coffee with Millie and Scott. Millie said, "Thought we were going to have to come look for you. We need to go back to my apartment to pick up your things before taking you to the airport."

"Millie, sorry to keep you waiting. I'm ready to go now. How about you, Drew? Are you ready?"

"Liz, I was ready over an hour ago. Been sitting here waiting on you and lover boy to finish your little chat," was Drew's reply.

Liz glared at Drew, and he knew she was not happy with his choice of words. Turning to face Steve, Liz reached out and gave him a hug. "Thank you for all you have done for Joanna. Seeing her like she is now has been such a blessing. But I do have one question concerning her. It's her speech. She is talking, but some words are hard for her. Can she overcome this in time?"

"I believe in time her speech will be better. We have been able to see an improvement in her in the last few weeks."

"Thanks again, Steve, for all you have done."

"What the doctors and I did for her was one thing, but her healing was by God's grace and mercy. Seeing the recovery she has made makes up for the long hours and many prayers that were given."

"Steve, you are really a great doctor. God has blessed you and your brother. I must go now and not keep Millie waiting. Come to Nashville whenever you get a chance."

"Liz, I have a feeling, I'll be in Nashville as often as I can. Have a safe flight home." Leaning over, Steve kissed Liz on the cheek and walked away.

Millie said, "Okay you guys, we must get going. I have to be back here soon for work."

Liz looked at Millie. "I thought you worked days. Have you gone to second shift?"

"No, I did some swapping around so I could be here for you. But come on, traffic at this time of day is bad. Come to think of it, traffic around here anymore is bad at any time."

Drew chuckled. "Have you forgotten how Nashville traffic is?"

"You have me on that one, but Raleigh is getting there."

Scott walked Millie, Drew, and Liz to the parking garage and told them goodbye. Rushing in at Millie's apartment, Liz and Drew picked up their things and headed to the airport. As Millie had said, traffic was terrible. They finally came to a complete stop. Traffic on both sides was not moving. After an hour, traffic began to pick up. When they arrived at the airport, Liz and Drew quickly told Millie goodbye, thanked her for her help, and took off running. They made it on the plane with five minutes to spare. Someone told Drew there had been a bad wreck that had traffic back up.

Drew nodded his head. "Yes, we sat in that traffic jam. Nothing moved."

Finally, they were back in Nashville. Dana was there to pick them up. She dropped Drew off first, then on the way to Liz's place, Dana asked. "So how was your trip?"

"Mom, it was so wonderful. I have a picture of Joanna and me. She is so beautiful, so loving and kind. Seeing her was a blessing. Also, I met a lady by the name of Beth McCloud. She and her husband are adopting Joanna."

"Liz, what kind of people are they?" Dana asked.

"Oh Mom, Beth is a wonderful lady. I felt like I already knew her, but I don't know where. They live in Lexington, Kentucky. I believe it's the right thing for them to adopt Joanna. Joanna needs them, and I feel they need her. I'll say, God is certainly in this, and it shows. One of the doctors that was so instrumental in her coming out of her coma was Dr. Steve Hunter."

Dana had just pulled into the parking lot at Liz's.

"You mean the Steve Hunter that came in with Millie and stayed at our house?"

"Yes. I had no idea he was working on Joanna's case, and I never realized what an outstanding doctor he is."

"It's a small world, Liz. I remember you had talked about Scott Hunter a long time ago. Did you know about Steve then?"

"No, I met Scott through a client. Then one day at the hospital, he saw me and recognized me. I mentioned Millie to him when I found out he worked at Duke, but the thought of ever seeing him again or that he had a brother that would be instrumental in helping Joanna never crossed my mind. It's so strange how you meet someone and don't realize that someday they can be a part of your life."

"That's why you should treat people with respect and love. You never know when they will come back into your life."

"You and daddy always told me that when I was a little girl. You said it was better to treat people the way you wanted to be treated than to treat them the way they should be, and that's so true. I know some of the cases I have handled, and I have had to remember that. Especially in Judge Mize's courtroom."

"Liz, have you ever regretted becoming an attorney?"

"No, Mom. I truly enjoy it. Take Millie, she would never make an attorney, but she's good in the medical field. You and Dad and Millie's parents are blessed. One daughter in the medical field and one in law."

"You're right, but I pray we never have to be in need of either one. Good night, Liz. Hope you sleep well."

"Good night, Mom. Thanks for the ride and for being here. You are the best and I love you very much." Liz gave her mom a hug before getting out of the car.

Seventeen

It had been two weeks and Liz had heard nothing from Steve or Millie. She had left Millie two messages, but no reply. Although Liz was trying to be patient, she still wanted to know how things were going in Raleigh. Chief Helton had agreed for her to stop wearing the monitor. He said it was against his better judgement, but Liz would not budge. She told him enough was enough. There had been no sign of Clarence Walters in months. Liz felt he had given up looking for Joanna, and she was sure moving her to North Carolina had been a good move in more than one way. She thought of Joanna but wanted to wait and let her make the first call. She was certain, being in a strange home and town with people she didn't know well, the child had a lot of adjusting to do. Sitting in her kitchen, having a second cup of coffee, Liz was letting her mind wander, and did not hear Gill walk in.

"You okay, Liz?"

"Yes, Gill. Just thinking. How are things going around here this morning?"

"You know. Liz, it amazes me at how many women are abused. As soon as we get a room empty, we have someone who needs it."

"Gill, I'm so thankful we have this place for them to go. I'm also so thankful for all the volunteers who put in so many hours. You guys are the ones that make this place possible."

You mean God. Liz, he touched our hearts and not a worker here can imagine not helping. Last night a lady called needing a place to go. A neighbor is bringing her and her two children here sometime today. She is coming from Georgia. Jana talked to her and is planning to put a baby bed in the room with the lady. The lady said the other child could sleep with her. According to Jana, it's a bad situation. "

"Gill, if you stop to think, all situations are bad. I don't understand why a man feels he must beat his wife and kids. If he's that unhappy, why doesn't he leave? I have heard so many stories and think nothing would surprise me, but occasionally, I'm taken aback by what I hear. You just never know."

"Liz, I could not do your job. I know I'm retired from security, but to do what you do? No, I would not make a good attorney. No one would want my services."

"That's why God made us all so different. I don't think I could do factory work, or be in the medical field, be a teacher, preacher, a singer, the list goes on. I don't even sing in the choir at church, for fear they would ask me to just pretend I'm singing."

"Liz, you can't be that bad. If you stand next to Mr. Roland, no one will know."

"Gill, that's terrible. Mr. Roland tries so hard. He puts his whole heart in singing."

"I know, but I made the mistake one Sunday and sat down beside him. No one around him could sing. I'm not sure which key he was on, but his voice carried out."

Laughing, Liz said. "I know, my Uncle Roy sat beside him one Sunday. He said, when the preacher was preaching, Mr. Roland would say, 'Yes', 'that's right' or quote the scripture during the whole service."

"Oh, he does. It's so distracting, but I will have to say this. If we ever need anything at the church, Mr. Roland is right there. He does more than his share. Always giving and giving from the heart. You can't help but love the old guy."

"How old is Mr. Roland, Gill?

"Gosh, Liz, I'm not sure, but he should be close to eighty-five, give or take a few years. But he is faithful. You can always count on him. You know, we are blessed to have Sam Roland. The church could use a few dozen like him."

"So, when he sings off key from now on, Gill, you can count your blessings, even sit beside him on Sundays?"

"Liz, that's what I like about you. Here I was thinking one way and now you have me thinking another, which is good. Guess we will just have to keep ole Mr. Roland around. Talk to you later, Liz."

Nina, Jana, and Liz worked most of the morning, getting ready for the family from Georgia. The lady bringing them said the woman brought very little with her. Apparently, she walked out of her home with the children, her purse, and a diaper bag. The little girl had a doll with her and that was it. Jana called around to collect some things they could use when they arrived. It was almost one-thirty when Sandy walked in. "They are here."

They all went downstairs to meet the new family. When they saw the woman, their hearts broke. You could tell she had taken a bad beating, and the little girl was holding her arm, as if it was hurting.

Liz walked over and said, "Hello, I'm Liz Barnett. Welcome to our home. We have lunch prepared if you would like to eat."

"Yes, that would be nice," the lady said. The baby was asleep, and Jana said. "We have a baby bed upstairs already for him if you don't mind me taking him up there. We have a room monitor here so you can hear if he wakes up."

The lady smiled and said, "That would be so nice." Jana took the little boy and carried him upstairs.

Nina was fixing them a plate of food when the lady asked, "Are you sure we are safe here?"

Liz smiled, "Yes, I am certain you are safe. I'm sorry, but I haven't been told your name or the children."

The lady was hesitant then finally said, "My name is Tammy Harrison, this is my daughter Tori, and my baby is Timmy. Can someone look at my daughter's arm? She says it hurts, but I wouldn't take her to the clinic for fear my husband would find out. I can't take her to a clinic here, either, because if they bill our insurance, he will know where we are."

Liz said, "Yes, we can have someone take a look at her and you. Is the baby, okay?"

"Yes, my husband didn't touch Timmy. Tori walked up to him when he was hitting me, and he turned on her. She doesn't cry, for he has told her if she cried, he would make it hurt worse."

Liz could feel her stomach cringe. Then she asked Tammy. "How old are your children?"

Tammy said with tears in her eyes, "Tori is three and Timmy is three months."

With that information, Nina walked out of the room to call the ladies on standby. She informed them of the children's ages and about what size they wore, along with the mother and that a doctor was needed to check both mother and daughter. In an hour, two ladies from the church came with some clothes, along with a doctor.

Liz informed Tammy who the people were and that they were her friends here to help. When they showed her the clothes and toys, Tammy broke down and cried. Dr. Shane Tolman walked over.

"Ma'am, I am Dr. Shane Tolman, I'm here to check you and your daughter over. I go to church with these ladies, and we offer our services at no cost to you. Whatever treatment you or your daughter may need will be our gift to you. You are in the house called 'Love by the Master' and that's what we do. We offer you our love because we care. Now, if you can tell me where you hurt, I'll take a look."

Again, tears rolled down Tammy's cheeks. "I'm sorry. I have never had anyone care for us like this. I don't know what to say."

Dr. Tolman patted her on the arm. "This is what God's children do. They look after those that need help. The Bible says we are to feed his sheep. You and your children are those little sheep that we are to look after and take care of. It's all done in love."

Tammy could not control her tears. Never had anyone shown her so much kindness.

"Could you check my daughter's arm first? I think I'm mostly bruised."

Dr. Tolman turned to Tori. "You are a very pretty little girl. Is that your doll?"

Tori only nodded.

"Do you mind if I look at your arm? I noticed you were holding it. Does it hurt?"

Again, Tori only nodded

Dr. Tolman barely touch the child's arm and she winced, but never said a word or cried.

The doctor gently examined her arm and was certain it was broken. Turning to Tammy he said, "I want to take her to the hospital to have her arm x-rayed. You will not be billed, and no one will know who she really is. We go to great lengths to protect our guests' identities. I'll bring her back to you as soon as we are finished, but before I leave, I need to check you."

He looked Tammy over carefully, and she had no broken bones, only bruises. Then he left with Tori.

Liz sat down and began to talk to Tammy about the place where she had found shelter. She explained that she and her children were safe and had no worries of being found. Nina took Mrs. Wallace, the neighbor, to a room to rest before heading back to Georgia. As Nina was leaving the room, Mrs. Wallace said to Nina, "I was told about this place through a friend. I had no idea such a place existed. You people are an answer to a prayer. Does Georgia have a home like this?"

"Not all states have places like this and if they do, you need to go to a place outside your state. It makes it safer. What happens here, stays here." Nina turned to leave.

"Thank you for what you are doing. I heard the doctor say you were never charged for being here. Do you take contributions?"

Smiling, Nina said, "That's what keeps this place going. It functions on love. 'GOD'S LOVE.' We have never had to worry about anything. God always supplies all our needs."

Mrs. Wallace smiled and said, "In the morning, I'll leave a check on the desk. I have never done anything like this before, and on my way here, I wondered why I was doing this. Now, I know. Mrs. Harrison and her children needed help, and for some reason, I felt the need to help them. I'm so thankful I didn't turn my back on them. This place has really touched my heart. I have never felt so much love in one place. How can I find out if Georgia has a place like this?"

Nina walked back over to Mrs. Wallace to give her a hug. "That's what God's children do. We have devotions every morning, and we would like it if you would join us before you leave. Also, you can speak with Liz. She can help you with that information."

"Thank you. I wouldn't miss it for the world. Now I know why this place is called 'Love by the Master.'"

Three hours later, Dr. Tolman came in with Tori. Her arm was in a cast. Tori went to her mom.

"Look Mom, they let me pick out the color I wanted for my cast. I picked pink and purple. The doctor here drew a heart on it and signed his name."

Tammy asked the Dr. Tolman. "Was it broken bad?"

"It was a clean break, so it will heal fine. I checked her over, and she has a few bruises, but her arm was the worst. She will heal and be in excellent shape in no time. I'll come by tomorrow and check on you both. I'm sure you are going to be pretty sore tomorrow, so if you can take a warm bath in some salts, that will help you. Liz has some on hand for situations such as this."

Tammy said, "Thank you. You have no idea how much this means to me."

"No worries. That is what we are here for. Sleep well and remember, you are very safe. No one can harm you or your children here." Then Dr. Tolman left.

After getting Tammy and Tori to bed, Liz went downstairs and thought about calling Millie again. No, she decided. She had already left several messages, she would wait.

The next morning as Liz was checking on Tammy and Tori, her phone rang. It was Beth McCloud.

"Hello, Beth. How are you and Joanna doing?"

"Hey, Liz. Wanted to let you know, we have enrolled Joanna in school here and she is doing fine. I know what the doctors told us about all she has gone through, and that school might be a bit much, but honestly, with the way she is, you would never have known it. That child is truly a miracle. She catches on so fast; I can't believe it. Even her speech is almost back to normal. With each passing day, I love her more and more. I was wondering, I know the doctors said you gave her the name Joanna. Do you know her given name?"

"I have nothing concrete, only speculation. Are you thinking of changing her name?"

"No, no, I think Joanna suits her fine. I was curious. She is doing so well, and if she should ever ask us about her previous family, I have nothing to tell her."

"To be honest, Beth, I am only guessing about what little I know. It may be correct, or it may not be correct. I don't want to pass on wrong information to you."

"Oh, I totally understand. If by any chance, you find anything out about her past, please let us know. I think it is important as she gets older for her to know."

"I certainly will, Beth. It's so good to hear from you and to know Joanna is doing so well. This is a big blessing."

As Liz hung up the phone, she looked up and said, "Lord, thank You. I know this is all because of You. I don't know the plans You have for that child, but I know You have something."

Mrs. Harrison came out of her room and saw Liz in the hall. "Ms. Barnett, may I talk to you?"

"Certainly. Would you like to talk in the kitchen over a cup of coffee?"

"Yes, that would be fine."

As they sat down, Tammy Harrison began to cry. "Miss Barnett, I need help. I have never felt so much love as I have felt here. I want whatever it is that you and your staff have. Is it very expensive and where do I go to get it?"

Smiling, Liz said, "Mrs. Harrison, it has been right at your fingertips all along. You see, God has been waiting patiently for you to ask him to be a part of your life. You are his child, and He loves you."

"Oh, Miss Barnett, I don't think He loves me. You see, I haven't been a very good person. I knew my husband had a drinking problem before we married, but I married him anyway. Well, really, I got pregnant before we got married. Things went from bad to worse and I kept thinking it would get better. My husband cheated on me, and when he gets drunk, things are really bad. When I got pregnant with Timmy, he was furious. Said it was all my fault and I would pay for it. I took the beatings till he started hitting Tori and I couldn't take that. Coming here things are so different. You can feel the difference when you walk in. I want that in my life, I want that for my children. Please, you have got to help me."

"Mrs. Harrison. God has always been with you. He has been waiting on you to ask Him into your heart. Let me read some scriptures to you."

By the time Liz had read the scriptures to Tammy and told her about Jesus, Tammy broke down and cried.

"You mean He will love someone like me?"

Liz put her arms around Tammy and said, "Oh, my child, God's love is an amazing love. No greater love will you ever find, than the love that God has."

Taking Tammy's hands and bowing her head, Liz prayed.

"Father, this daughter of yours, Tammy, is repenting of her sins and surrendering her life to you. Wash her, dear Lord and, cleanse her. Create in her a clean heart. Give her a new life that is abundant and free. As it says in Romans 10:9 *'If you confess with your mouth that Jesus is Lord and believe in your heart that God raised Him from the dead, you will be saved.'* You know Father, that in Romans 3:23, it says, *'For all have sinned and fall short the glory of God.'* I lift this child up to you today, Father. Help her, Lord, as she walks the path she has never walked before."

As Liz finished praying, Rod Dotson walked in. When she looked up, she knew God had sent him at the perfect time. She introduced Rod to Tammy and left them alone. She walked back into the room about thirty minutes later to find out Tammy wanted to be baptized and start her life over. Mrs. Wallace was getting ready to leave when she heard the news about Tammy. Walking into the kitchen where Tammy and Pastor Rod were, she said, "This trip has been a trip I'm so grateful for. God has opened my eyes. I'm taking back to Georgia something special that only could come from God. Here is my donation to this beautiful place. I will never forget what 'Touched by the Master' has done for me. Thank you so very much." Hugging Tammy, and Liz, Mrs. Wallace left to go home to Georgia.

Eighteen

anting to help Tammy in every way possible, Liz had a friend of hers check out Tammy's husband. Sure enough, he was unable to keep a job and what money he did earn, he spent on alcohol.

Preparing the divorce papers, Liz had her friend serve the papers on Jon Harrison. When he was approached about the divorce papers, he laughed and said sure, he would sign them.

He never asked about his wife or children. For all he knew, they were still somewhere in Georgia.

Having turned her life around, Tammy was like a totally different person. Even Tori was acting more like a little three-year-old girl.

Liz was still playing phone tag with Millie. It seemed they were never free to talk at the same time. Wondering what was going on in Raleigh, Liz still refused to call Steve. She still was back and forth on her feelings. If only she could talk to Millie. That evening, just as Liz was getting ready for bed, her phone rang. It was Millie.

"Millie, I can't believe we are finally getting to talk."

"Hey, Liz. It has been pretty wild up here, so much going on. How are things your way?"

"About the same. How are things with you and Scott?"

"That's why I am calling. Scott and I are getting married. It will be a small wedding, but I want you to be here."

"Millie, this is great. Have you set a date yet?"

"Yes, it will be in three months, so I need you to go ahead and keep your calendar clear for that week. I called Mom and Dad, and they are so excited. I had to get a little stern with Mom because she started saying she would do this and that, not once did she take the time to listen to what I was saying. Finally, I told her we were getting married here, not in Nashville, and the wedding was to be small. I explained that Scott and I had already decided what kind of wedding we wanted, and we would take care of everything. All she had to do was come."

"So, how did that go over?" Liz asked.

"To be honest, not good. She started with a thousand and one questions, and I finally told her, Mom, we are going to do this our way. When we hung up, she probably went over to your moms and started crying."

"I appreciate the heads up, for I have both our moms to deal with."

"Liz, I want you to be my maid of honor. I'll send you a picture of what kind of dress I want you to wear and the color. We are planning an outdoor wedding, and the venue is beautiful."

"You know, Millie, I wouldn't miss this for the world. Will I be your only attendant?"

"Yes, like I said, it will be small. Scott and I both know so many people, so we decided not to worry about who to invite, just keep it family and some special friends. The week of my wedding, I want you to come and stay here with me. I'm taking the week off and I want us to spend that time together."

"Will you not be trying to get set up on where you will be living and all that?"

"No, Liz, Scott has already bought a house. He and Steve have been working getting it all ready. In fact, they are living in it, and I have a friend that I work with that wants my place, so when the house is finished, what little I want to keep I will send over to the house. When we get married, all we will have to do is move in."

"Millie, you, and Scott have really gotten this together. This is wonderful."

"This time, Liz, I'm doing things right. Scott and I both agree that marriage is sacred. He is so godly, so loving, so respectful of me. I know without a doubt that God's blessing is in this marriage. Everything seems so right, so perfect. You have no idea how many times I have thanked God for giving me a second chance and I don't deserve it. Before, I treated my family so bad, and in turn, I was treated even worse, but God has given me the best man on this earth. Scott and I both agree that God is first in our life, and we are second."

"Millie, I am so happy for you and Scott. I wouldn't worry about Aunt Debbie, she will come around, for she likes Scott."

"I know she is upset because I won't let her do all the planning, but this is our wedding. She and Dad decided on how they wanted their wedding, and I want the same."

"Well, Millie, their wedding was a little different. It was a double wedding. I'm sure our dads had little if anything to say about it."

"Liz, that's it. You and Steve could marry when Scott and I do. We could have a double wedding also."

"First of all, Steve and I are not engaged, in fact we seldom talk. Also, he lives in one state and I live in another. Big, big difference."

"You know, Liz, you could call him."

"If Steve wants to talk to me, he will call."

"Liz, he has explained how he feels about you. You are the one holding back. It's not his fault you are being so stubborn. Maybe at the wedding you will catch the bouquet, and he will catch the garter."

"Funny, Millie. I'll be at the wedding, but I won't be out front trying to catch the bouquet. So, send me the information about the dress and I'll see what I can do."

"Go ahead, change the subject, but know, I'm working on more than just my wedding."

"Good-night, Millie. Love you."

Lying in bed, Liz wondered about Steve. She also wondered what Millie would be up to. Only time would tell.

Sandy Leonard called Liz at work. "Hate to bother you while at work, but I thought you might want to know this. A friend from church said a family in Texas has a large ranch and is looking for workers. They need a housekeeper, and they were told about Tammy Harrison. The lady called here to talk to Tammy, and she will be flying here next week to take Tammy and her children to Texas."

"Oh, my. So, Tammy wants to move to Texas?"

"It seems the couple has children also, and they feel this would be good for both of them. They have a room at the back of their house where Tammy and the children can stay."

"You know, Sandy, this is good, for it will give Tammy and her children more of home life. Has anyone checked out this family to make sure this is a good move?"

"Yes, Mrs. Lawson at church knows this family well and highly recommends the move. Seems they are well known in Dallas, Texas, and a godly family."

"Good, if Mrs. Lawson approves this, then it must be a good move. I'm happy for Tammy, she deserves a good chance in life. Thanks, Sandy, for letting me know. See you tonight at the house."

As Liz pondered over Sandy's call, she thought back at how many women had come to her home for shelter and how many had been able to leave happier and more stable. She could only recall one lady that refused to accept God, come to their Bible studies, or have prayer with them. They all had tried so hard to help her, but her heart was so hard. She left one day and no one knew where she went or whatever happen to her. Still, from time to time, Liz would offer up a prayer for her.

Three months went by quickly. Liz had her dress and loaded up her car to head to Raleigh. She and Millie had talked several times but neither one ever mentioned Steve. The drive would do Liz good; it would give her time to think what she would say when she saw Steve. She still had some feelings for him, but Satan was so good about putting so many doubts in her mind. How many times had she prayed for an answer?

Pulling up at Millie's apartment, Liz got out and unloaded her suitcase. When she got to the door, Steve opened it.

"Here, let me help you with your things."

Not expecting to see him this soon, she asked, "Where's Millie?"

"She and Scott received a phone call and had to leave to take care of a matter. How was the drive?"

"It was good. Long, but good. How are you doing, are you ready for the big wedding?"

"I'm doing great, staying very busy. I have some things I'm working on. Between helping Scott and Millie and with work, I have very little free time."

"Yes, Millie said you were helping Scott fix up their home. I bet it looks good."

"I think so. I would take you there, but I'm sure they want to be the ones to show you their place. Wouldn't do for me to spoil that for them. Do you have any more luggage to bring in? If so, I can go get it?"

"Just my dress for the wedding. I can get it. Thanks."

Walking out to her car, Liz thought seeing Steve was not what she was planning. At least not this soon. Everything she had thought about saying to him in the car seem to vanish. She couldn't recall a single thought. Seeing him had messed all that up. Even talking to him did something to her. She really needed to pull herself together. Gathering up her dress, Liz took a deep breath and started back to the apartment.

Millie and Scott were gone nearly two hours. Liz and Steve made small talk. When they finally arrived, Millie walked over to Liz.

"I'm so happy you are here. The four of us are going to have a great week."

Liz tried not to look surprised. She had though she and Millie were going to spend the week together before the wedding. What had changed? Now it was to be the four of them. How was she ever going to get through this week with Steve around so much?

True to her word, Millie had planned something every day for the four of them. Finally, the day of the wedding arrived. Debbie, Roy, Dana, and Ryan were staying at a hotel not far from the wedding venue.

Millie's dress was an off-white, ankle-length dress. Liz's dress was light blue and ankle length. Scott wore a black tux, as well as Steve and Roy, with a light blue cummerbund. Debbie's dress was a mixture of cream and light blue.

When Liz walked down the aisle, she could feel Steve looking at her. Keeping her eyes ahead, she refused to look his way. After the ceremony, they were all to go to Scott and Millie's new home for the reception. Doing everything she could to avoid Steve, Liz felt the day would never end. The week had not been so bad, she just hadn't planned on spending every day with him. Although Millie said that she and Scott had thought it would be great for the four of them to spend that week together, Liz thought it would have been better if the week had been for her and Millie, without the guys.

It was time for the bride and groom to leave on their honeymoon trip to the Bahamas. When it came time for Millie to throw her bouquet, Liz made sure she stayed in the house. Steve walked in, "Millie is looking for you."

"Tell her I'll be out soon. I wanted to pick up in here first."

Steve walked over to Liz and picked her up. "Millie is waiting on you so she can throw her bouquet. Let's not hold things up."

He carried Liz outside where everyone was waiting patiently on her. She could feel her face turning every shade of red possible. Setting her down, he smiled. "Hope you catch the bouquet!"

As he walked away, Liz turned just as Millie threw her bouquet and it landed perfectly in Liz's arms. Everyone began to clap. Dana walked over to her daughter. "Oh, Liz. This means you will be the next bride!"

There were six other girls standing by to try to catch the bouquet and it just happen to fall in Liz's hands. What luck.

Then Scott was getting ready to throw the garter. As Steve passed Liz, he said, "Hope I'm as lucky as you were."

Nine guys gathered around to try to catch the garter. Steve was a good head taller than all of them and he snatched that garter without a problem. Looking for Liz, he spotted her and held up the garter and smiled. Liz managed a smile and thought, no way are we getting married. Too many miles between us.

As Millie and Scott left for the airport, Steve got a called from the hospital. It was an emergency and they apologized for having to call him. Steve told Liz, I am sorry, but I need to go to the hospital." With that, he left.

Soon the house was all cleaned up and back in order. Liz spent the night at Millie's apartment and headed back to Nashville early the next morning. Steve had not called, nor did she try to call him. She was about two hours from home when her phone rang. It was Steve.

"Hey, Liz. Sorry I wasn't able to get back with you sooner, but there was a bad emergency and I needed to take care of it. I went by Millie's just now and saw you had already gone. I had wanted to tell you goodbye."

"I understand, Steve. You're a doctor and it's your job to save lives."

"I was hoping we could talk. Seemed like someone was always around, and we never had any time to ourselves."

"I know. It has been a busy week, but the wedding was beautiful. I know Scott and Millie are going to be so happy. Before I forget, will you let Millie know I left the spare key under the rock in the flower bed?"

"Liz, we need to talk, and not over the phone. I can't get away right now, but as soon as I can clear my schedule, I'll fly to Nashville. See you soon."

Liz heard a click. Steve never indicated what it was he wanted to talk about. Was it about them, or had he found someone in Raleigh? For the next two hours, Liz's mind went from one thing to another.

Nearly a month had passed, and all Liz received from Steve were a few text messages, which she replied to him briefly. Giving Millie time to settle down, she called to see how married life was treating her.

"Oh, Liz. Scott is the best husband in the whole world. I don't know when I have been happier. Have you had a chance to talk to Steve lately?"

"No, he sends a text once in a while and that's about it."

"I'm surprised, he has time to send a text. Dr. Warren, the one that took such an interest in Steve and worked so hard in helping him be the doctor he is today, was in a bad car wreck the day we married. Steve has practically worked around the clock. They weren't sure Dr. Warren or his wife were going to make it. Steve is so sleep deprived; I don't know how he is functioning."

"Millie, I had no idea. Steve never said a word about this in his text."

"Dr. Warren took Steve under his wing and taught him so much. Dr. Reagan had a heart attack two days after Dr. Warren's wreck and Dr. Cameron is off on a month's vacation in Australia. He has no idea what is going back here, and Steve is trying to play superhero and seeing all the patients that normally four doctors see. I'm afraid he is going to collapse. Liz, why don't you call Steve? I know he would love to hear from you and maybe it would take his mind off all he is going though for a few minutes."

"I hate to bother him with all that he has on his plate."

"Liz, what are you afraid of? Honestly, to be such a smart attorney, you can be so dumb at times."

"Thank you, Millie. You really know how to make a person feel good."

"No, seriously, Liz. Steve is crazy about you, and you treat him like dirt. What gives?"

"I don't want to build his hopes up about us. Like I have told you before, he lives in Raleigh, and I live in Nashville. For a while I thought it would work but it won't. We both need to move on."

"Liz Barnett, you must be the most stubborn, hardheaded person I know. I love you, but you have blinders on and refuse to take them off. Scott and I have been praying for you and Steve. Maybe you should too."

"Millie, I have prayed about this. You need to let this go. I do hope Steve gets some rest and the doctors both recuperate very soon."

"That's it? This is all you have to say?"

"Millie, I wish you and Scott well. Love you. Bye."

Liz knew Millie was probably fuming right now and knew she was not going to give up. She was already dreading the next call from Millie.

year had passed, and Liz and Steve were still just good friends. Millie had let up on giving Liz a hard time about seeing Steve, but still when the family all got together, Steve was always there. He got along so well with both families and though nothing was said, Liz could tell by the way her parents acted, they thought the world of Steve. Pouring herself into her work, Liz had little time to think about him and what if. Dealing with Chief Helton and Judge Mize was enough for Liz. Things at home seem to go smoothly. She had the same staff, and everyone knew what to do. It was so nice to come home and find letters from women who had previously been at the shelter. To see how they had moved on with their lives and how they thanked her and the staff for their guidance.

That night as Liz looked through the mail, she found a letter that was postmark from Kentucky. No return address but being from Kentucky, she automatically thought of Joanna. Opening it, she saw it was from Joanna and not Beth McCloud. It read:

Dear Miss Barnett,

I think of you often and I have our picture sitting on my nightstand. I am in school and with the help of a tutor that my wonderful parents hired to help me, I am doing very well. All my studies come so easily for me, which is a miracle considering how long I was in a coma. I took a test a few weeks ago to see what level I am at, and it came back that I was functioning on the level of a freshman in college. I plan on going to medical school. I have a desire to help others, for so many people did so much to help me. I want to ask you something. Not sure if you will be able to help, but I don't know anyone else to ask.

I have been having dreams lately, and in all my dreams I am a little girl. I can see a woman's face but can't make out her features. Sometimes she speaks to me, and I think it is my mother. The best I can remember, my mother went away when I was little. I know you had done some research in trying to find my parents, and I was wondering if you had found anything out that would help me. Maybe explain why I keep seeing this lady and if it could be my mother? I don't have any dreams of a man and I don't know where my father is, either. For some reason, I am unable to form a picture of either one of them in my mind. I'm not sure if this is good or bad, since I can't remember anything about my childhood, other than at times it's like I can hear my daddy say things to me. This mostly happens when I have these dreams about a woman. It's like I hear a voice say she has left and not coming back.

My mama Beth McCloud said God may be protecting me from something bad, the reason I can't remember. If you have any information to share that you think would help me, I would greatly appreciate it. If the information you have would bring me heartache, then I ask that you don't share that with me. I have prayed and asked God to let me see the woman's face more clearly and in time, maybe He will.

I pray this letter finds you not only in good health but with great happiness. You will always hold a special place in my heart, for because of you, I know about God and what a wonderful a person He is. You gave me a very special gift for which I will be eternally grateful.

Much Love,
Your Kentucky Girl
Joanna McCloud

As Liz finished reading the letter, she thought back about what Chief Helton had said about Clarence Walters and his daughter Carrie. Nothing was ever proven that Joanna was really Carrie, and then right out of the blue, Mr. Walters disappeared. Should she share with Joanna the what-ifs or should she let sleeping dogs lie? Reaching for her Bible, she searched the scriptures for an answer. She spent the next two hours reading and searching but came up with nothing.

Praying always helped, but as Liz tried to pray, it was as if she had a block. What was wrong? What was she missing?

The next morning, she called Pastor Rod and asked if she could speak with him. She was to meet him around eleven. Arriving at the church a little early, Liz went into the sanctuary. She went all the way down to the front and just stood there. With her eyes closed, she began to pray for the meeting with Pastor Rod. When he arrived, he motioned for Liz to follow him to his office.

"Morning, Liz. I know you have something on your mind for it shows in your face and has for some time."

Looking surprised, Liz said, "I'm here over a letter I received yesterday in the mail. What do you mean by the look on my face?"

"Let's take one thing at a time. Would you like to discuss the letter first?"

"Yes, that's why I'm here." Handing him the letter, she waited till he had read the letter before she said anything.

Then she explained about the information from Chief Helton, her wearing the monitor and now the disappearance of Mr. Walters. "I tried to pray about this last night, even search the scriptures, but for some reason, I feel nothing. I can't explain my feelings."

"Liz, remember I said you have had something on your mind for a long time, for it showed in your face? The reason you are struggling now is you are not facing your own problems. You can't bury them and go on. You are a wonderful Christian, but even sometimes, we bury our problems and concentrate on helping others. Until you get things right with yourself, you are going to find it harder and harder to communicate with God. It's not that He doesn't care about us, it's His way of opening our eyes. We need Him and when we realize something is wrong, we must bow down and search ourselves. I'm sure you have read Psalm 139.

The whole chapter is wonderful, but in verse twenty-three and twenty-four it says:

"Search me, O God, and know my heart; test me and know my anxious thoughts. See if there is any offensive way in me and lead me in the way everlasting."

"But Rod, I don't know of anything I'm hiding. I try so hard to do right at the shelter and at work, I do my best for my clients."

"Liz, what about you? What are you holding deep inside of you? Once you deal with it, I feel you will be able to pray again and feel God's presence. You know He hasn't left you; He is waiting for you to take care of some things and only you can do that. I know this wasn't the answer you were expecting, but ever since you called, I have been praying and this is what God is telling me. I even have to get away alone and search myself at times. We get so caught up in all we do that we overlook ourselves."

Liz sat quietly, not sure what to say. Rod was right, this was not what she was expecting to hear. She came here about Joanna, not herself.

Reaching his hands across his desk, he said, "Liz let's pray, for you have some work to do. Go somewhere alone and pour your heart out to God. Be patient and listen. When this is done, you will be able to pray about your letter."

Taking hold of Rod's hands, Liz had a feeling come over her that she had never felt. She realized at that moment; he was right. Bowing their heads, he prayed for Liz.

When they finished praying, Liz thanked Pastor Rod and went back to the sanctuary. Looking around she remembered so many times she had come to the church asking prayer for a home, then about taking in people needing a safe place to stay. Then asking them to pray for a bigger home, for hers had become too small. She also had asked if anyone would like to volunteer to help at her shelter. Every request, God had provided. She even requested special prayer for Joanna. As she looked around, tears began to fall down her cheeks. She knelt at the altar and cried out to her precious Father.

"Oh Father, here I am. Show me what I need to do. Show me where I have failed You. I need You so much, please Father, for whatever I have not done, forgive me. Help me to make things right. If I have wronged anyone, show me, whatever it is, I may not like it, but I want to be cleansed and walk closer to you. Here I am, Lord, take this old body of clay and reshape it to be the servant You would have me be."

Pastor Rod heard someone in the sanctuary, and when he walked in, he saw Liz. Turning, he closed the door to give her this time alone with God. She was where she needed to be, and he knew she would find her answers.

Twenty

A month had gone by, and one Saturday morning, Liz called Joanna. When she answered, she was so bubbly. Her voice was even stronger than the last time they had spoken.

"Miss Barnett, it is so good to hear from you, how are you?"

"Joanna, I am good and from the sound of your voice, things must be going well for you."

"Oh, they are. I have taken some tests and I'm waiting to hear to see if I have been accepted into med school."

"Well, this is wonderful. I am so proud of you."

"Like I told you in my letter, I had a tutor, and once I understood some things, my mind took off. I read books that are for college students and even have been reading medical books. I understand it all and find it so interesting. My mind retains all that I read."

"Joanna, you are amazing."

"Miss Barnett, I owe it all to you. You were there to give me hope and encouragement. With your love, support, and kind words, it was as if you knew what I needed. You never gave up."

"My dear, it was God that was with you."

"But I don't ever remember hearing about God or knew what prayer was till then. My parents now are outstanding parents.

They are like you, so encouraging. They can't believe how far advanced in my studies I am."

"How old are you, Joanna?" asked Liz.

"They are guessing I am around eighteen. I don't ever remember a birthday. I keep praying my memory will come back. Oh, by the way, do you know anything about my past?"

"What little Chief Helton found out, and we are not hundred percent sure you are the same person in question. The child he was told about did not have a very good life. We don't know who dropped you off at my door or why. Still so many unanswered questions. The main thing is you have made a marvelous recovery and been blessed with a wonderful family."

"That still doesn't answer the face in my dreams."

"Are you still having those dreams?"

"Yes, and the woman is saying something to me, but I can't understand her. It's so strange that no one knows who I am or where I came from and why I'm having these dreams."

"Be patient, Joanna. In time, God may reveal things to you. You may get some or all of your memory back. Think of it like this, God may be protecting you, and you need to move on. There is a reason, trust God for he knows what's best for you."

"I know you are right, but sometimes I can't help but wonder who I really am. I have wondered if I was kidnapped and maybe my other parents are looking for me. Do I have any siblings? Are my parents dead? It's like some days, the questions don't go away. I try to fill all my time studying and this seems to help, then when I go to bed, here comes all these questions. Not every night but most nights.

"When the questions come, read your Bible, and turn it over to God. He will guide you. Remember, He is always with you. Day and night, always on call. He is your very best friend."

"Miss Barnett, I love you. Hearing you talk, I can close my eyes and remember you talking to me when I was in the hospital. You have such a soothing voice."

"Joanna, call me anytime. I will always be here for you."

Liz could not believe how well Joanna was doing. She also understood why she wanted to know about her past. What little she told her was all she felt she needed to say at the present time.

Another month had passed when Liz received a call from Steve while she was at work. She was getting ready to go to court when he called. Liz knew she didn't have much time to talk, yet she hated not to answer her phone.

"Good morning, Steve. How are you doing today?"

"Liz, I am well, thank you. I know you are probably busy, but I was wondering if you had plans for dinner tonight?"

"Are you going to be in Nashville?" she asked, not expecting this.

"I'm in Nashville now, Liz, and was wondering if you'd like to have dinner with me if you don't have other plans."

"No, I don't have any plans." She said hesitantly.

"Wonderful, I'll pick you up at your place, say six o'clock?"

"Sure, that will be fine." Liz heard a click on her phone. She was shocked that Steve had called her and even more shocked that he was in town. It suddenly dawned on her that he said he would pick her up. Had he driven to Nashville, or had he borrowed one of her parents' cars? Did her parents know Steve was coming and failed to tell her? This was not good; here she was getting ready to go to court with so many unsettled questions on her mind. As soon as she got a break, she would give her mom a call. Knowing how much they like Steve, she wouldn't put it past them to have picked him up at the airport, loaned him a car, and even let him stay with them without saying a word to her.

Court seemed to go on and on. When they did take a ten-minute break, Liz was unable to call anyone. At four-thirty, Liz walked back into her office and the first thing she did was call her mom. It went to her voice mail, so Liz called her dad. Same thing. So, she called his shop and Uncle Roy answered.

"Uncle Roy, this is Liz. Do you by any chance know where my parents are? I have called both phones and no answer."

"Your dad is outside helping a customer and I think your mom and Debbie are at the church doing some work. They left out this morning and said they would be gone all day. Anything wrong?"

"No, all is well. It just gave me a little scare when neither one answered their phone!"

"Don't you worry, they are both fine. How are you doing?"

"You know me, always staying busy. Say hello to Aunt Debbie for me. Talk to you later."

As Liz hung up the phone, she thought to herself, apparently my parents don't know Steve is in town. I wonder why he is in Nashville. Something didn't seem right. She thought about calling Millie, then decided against it. Then she wondered if things were okay with Scott and Millie. The only thing she could do was wait till tonight to see what Steve wanted.

Traffic was terrible and seemed only to get worse. She found herself leaving for work earlier in the morning and getting home later in the evening. When she pulled in her driveway, there was Steve standing by a car, waiting for her.

"Sorry if I'm late, but traffic was extremely bad coming home."

"No worries, Liz. I'm early, so take your time. If you need to go in and check on things, go ahead. I made dinner reservations for us, and we have plenty of time."

"Thanks, let me check to make sure everything is running smoothly. Care to come in?"

Before they went inside, Liz notice, the tags on Steve's car was from North Carolina. So, he had driven in. Her mind was going in so many directions. Why was he here? Gill met her at the door.

"Hey, Liz. I was on my way out. We have a full house tonight, and everyone is settled in. Jana and Myra will be here till you get back. Have a good dinner."

"Gill, how did you know I was going out for dinner tonight?"

"Steve came by this morning to make sure there would be coverage for you tonight. You know we will take care of you. Got to go, enjoy your evening."

Turning to Steve, Liz said, "You came by here this morning?"

"Yes. I wanted to make sure you didn't have to worry about things here and that you have a nice relaxing evening. Hope you don't mind."

"Am I missing something here? You call this morning to ask me for dinner tonight, and I find out you are already in town and now you clear my evening for me?"

"Is that so wrong of me?"

"I'm not sure. I'm not use to anyone planning my evening like this," was all Liz could say. Her mind was filling up with so many unanswered questions, she wasn't sure what question to ask first.

"Why don't you relax and enjoy the evening? You look very nice. I would never guess you had been in court all day."

Wanting to change the subject, Liz asked, "You said you made dinner reservations?"

"Yes, the place I chose came highly recommended. I hope you will like it."

"You're not familiar with Nashville, do you know how to get there?" she asked.

"Yes, the guys took me by there this afternoon so I would know where to go."

"So, you are here with a group of other doctors?"

"No, I came on my own. It was a nice drive."

Liz realized Steve was not going to give her any more information than he had to. She hated to keep asking more questions.

Steve took her by the arm. "If you're ready, shall we go?"

Liz began to wonder if they were meeting up with another group of doctors. They were probably married, and Steve needed a dinner partner, but then why would he be dining with other doctors, here in Nashville? Maybe they had a case where someone was in a coma, but then they wouldn't discuss this over dinner, surely. Liz and Steve made small talk as he drove to the restaurant. Still, Liz was trying to figure out why he was in Nashville.

Steve pulled in at the Kayne Prime Steak House. "Have you ever eaten here before?"

"No, I haven't but have heard the food here is very good. Did your friends comment on how the food was?"

"Yes," was all he said.

Once inside, they were greeted by the maître d'. "Evening Dr. Hunter. Your table is ready for you sir."

Liz turned to look at Steve, wondering how the maître d' knew who he was. What was she missing? Steve took her arm and led her to a table that was away from everyone. Liz had to admit, it was very nice.

Once seated, Steve said, "I took the liberty of ordering our dinner ahead. I hope you will enjoy what I chose."

Not use to all this, Liz smiled and said, "I'm sure I will, this is a very nice restaurant. Did you see the line of people when we walked in?"

"Yes, that's why I reserved a table and preordered our dinner."

They made small talk during dinner and when the waiter brought out dessert, Liz asked if she could have a to-go box, for she wanted to eat it later. Steve did the same. As they were leaving, the line to go in was still rather lengthy. When they got ready to get in the car, Steve asked Liz, "Would you like to go for a walk in the park? It's a really nice evening."

"Sure, after that wonderful meal, walking would be good for us."

The park was not very far away, and Liz always enjoyed going there. Once they arrived, they found it was not crowded at all, for which they were grateful. Again, they made small talk as they walked. Coming upon a bench, Steve asked, "Mind if we sit and talk?"

As they sat down, Steve turned to Liz and said, "I have been here in Nashville all week. I'll be going back home day after tomorrow."

Liz looked at him. "You have been here all week and just now letting me know?"

"I have been here on business. This is really the first chance I have had to get out and I had wanted to spend my free evening with you. I also wanted to make sure of some things. You see, I have been offered a job here at Vanderbilt University. If I take the position, I will be over the Neurologist Center. I have talked to Dr. Warren at Duke, for I really like it there, but I have gone as far as I can go until he or Dr. Regan or Dr. Cameron retires and that will not be anytime soon. Dr. Warren has been advising me on some things. He has my best interest at heart, and I appreciate his guidance and advice, for he is the one who took me under his wing and helped me to be the doctor I am today."

"Steve, this is wonderful. Do you think you will accept the position?"

"This is why I wanted to have dinner with you tonight. You have always said, due to the distance between us, we could only be friends. You never did want to make any kind of a commitment. If I am here, I need to know where I will stand in your life."

Liz didn't comment. She sat there looking at the ground as Steve talked.

"Liz, you don't have to give me an answer now. I want you to think about this and be honest with your feelings. What is your heart telling you? Maybe you have someone else in your life and I would be in the way. I will call you in a week, and hopefully this will give you some time to decide what you want. You know how I feel about you. Nothing has changed, but this can't be one sided. We both have to want the same thing. Keep in mind, being a doctor, the hours are long and very unpredictable. I have taken an oath to do my best to heal the sick. God is first in my life, my patients next and then my family. You need to know this up front."

"So, you are taking this position here at Vanderbilt?"

"Do you want me to?"

Again, Liz did not comment. So many things were going through her mind, and then Pastor Rod's statement came to her. He said she needed to search deep inside, for there was something she wasn't dealing with, and she needed to. Until she did, she would not find the peace she was looking for. Not realizing Steve was talking to her, Liz looked up. "I'm sorry, something you said, made me think of something else. Thank you, I do need some time to think."

Steve could tell by looking at Liz something was troubling her. He was not sure if it was him or what he had said to her, but she was carrying a very heavy burden.

"If you like, I can take you home now."

"Yes, thanks, I would like that."

The drive back to Liz's was very quiet. Neither said a word. When they pulled in, Steve got out to open the door for Liz and walked her to the house. Leaning over, he kissed her on the forehead.

"I enjoyed dinner," he said, handing Liz her dessert. "I will call in about a week." Turning he walked back to his car.

Liz went inside and all was quiet. Walking to her bedroom, she could feel tears rolling down her cheeks. The one thing she had not truly prayed about was her relationship with Steve. She knew how he felt about her, but she basically left him hanging. She hadn't come face to face with what she needed to do. This was why she felt God had closed a door on her. Falling on her knees by her bed, Liz cried out to God for help.

Sitting in his car, Steve felt a burden for Liz. He knew which room was hers, so he got out of his car, walked over, and stood under the window and began to pray. He was honest with her when he said God was first in his life, then his patients, then family. He gave God full credit in being the doctor he was. All through school, med school, he always prayed and asked for God to guide him. He also took time to thank God. With every patient, he always mentioned what an awesome God we have and if he knew a patient was lost, he took extra time to tell them about the God he served. As Steve prayed, he asked that God speak to Liz. If she didn't have the same feelings as he had, to make it known. He wanted a help mate that met God's approval.

The next morning, Liz was tired. It had been a long night. Around five that morning, she felt God speaking to her. She had been so lost without Him, and now though tired, she felt alive again. Life without God was no life at all. She never wanted to go through this again. Her thoughts were so much clearer. As she worked in the kitchen that morning, she felt like she was floating. Jana walked in and when she looked at Liz, she smiled.

"Welcome back, Liz."

Turning to Jana, Liz asked, "What do you mean welcome back? I haven't gone anywhere."

"Yes, you have. Seeing you this morning is like having the old Liz back. Don't know what has happened, but you are yourself again." Jana walked over and gave Liz a hug. "We have all been concerned about you, and seeing you this morning is an answer to our prayers. God is good."

"I didn't know you were able to see a change in me. Why didn't someone say something?"

"We took it to God, for we didn't want you to feel we were prying into your life. Also, we were not sure what to say. We made the right choice and let God handle it."

With tears in her eyes, Liz said, "Jana, I left God out of a very important thing in my life. It was as if He had closed the door on me. Last night, the one thing I had not asked Him about, I took it to Him and laid it all out. This morning, He opened that door. I felt God's arms around me again. I had missed Him so much. I pray I never do this again."

"Liz, you are only human. We all do this from time to time and later wonder what we were thinking. God was letting you know He is still in charge and how much He is needed. We have to humble ourselves, and when in that valley, there is only one way up and that is to turn to God."

"Jana, I thought I had, but I left out one thing when I was trying to rid myself of any issues that I had."

"God knew you had to face that issue and until you did, you would be miserable. Others could see something was wrong, but it was between you and God. He is patient Liz, and I'm so grateful He is."

"Thanks Jana, for listening to me."

"Liz, look at how God has blessed you. He knows you are one of his and He uses us to help each other and others."

"Jana, after breakfast, I have something I need to take care of. Hopefully, I won't be long. Anything we need while I'm out?"

"No, we are fine. Liz, it's so good to see that happiness in your eyes and on your face. I'm glad it was my day to come in."

After breakfast and the morning devotions were done, Liz left to take care of her errand. She went to Vanderbilt University to see if she could find Steve. She knew what she needed to say to him and wanted it to be face to face and not over the phone. When she arrived, she asked if they could have him page since she was sure he was somewhere in the hospital. Waiting in the hospital patient lounge, the receptionist came over and said, "I was told he was not in the hospital." Thanking her, Liz walked outside, not wanting to call him, but she didn't know what else to do. As she looked up his number, she heard someone say, "Liz, is everything alright? What are you doing here?"

Looking up it was Pastor Rod. "Oh, morning, I was here to see a friend. I guess you are here making your hospital visits."

"No, I am here for another reason. I am early though, with traffic like it is, I had rather be early than late. How are things going with you?"

"To be honest, much better. I did what you said, but not all at once. Took a while."

"Liz, we have a tendency to want to hang on to some things and not let it all go. It's those lessons that stick with us. If things were easy, we wouldn't remember them so well."

"How well, I have found out. When you feel separated from God, it's a terrible feeling, then when you get Him back in your life, you appreciate Him so much."

"Liz, I knew you were going through something, and it's a blessing to see what you let God do for you. Take care and we will see you Sunday."

As Pastor Rod walked away, Liz was so thankful for his advice. In her line of work, she was always giving people advice. Who would have ever thought her life would take a turn like it did? As she walked toward her car, Steve pulled in right beside where she was parked. Getting out of his car, he looked at her.

"Liz, I wasn't expecting to see you here."

"I know. I didn't call you, because I wanted to talk to you face to face and not over the phone. I took a chance that I would be able to see you."

Steve looked at his watch. "I have about twenty minutes before my meeting, do you want to talk here? There's a sitting area not far from here if you want to walk there to talk."

"No, I don't want to keep you or make you late for your meeting. I gave a lot of thought about what you said last night, and I did a lot of praying about it. I have an answer for you. I don't need a week to make my decision and I want to be honest with you. You have been very up front with me, and I have made all kinds of excuses, why we can't be together. You see, in the last little while, I felt like God had closed the door on my life. I had laid so many things out before Him, except one thing, and that was us. I turned it all over to Him this morning and then He gave me my answer. Steve, I do care for you very much and having you here close by will change everything. I would like nothing more than to spend more time with you and get to know you better. As for your commitment, God should always be first, your patients next and as for me, God will work that out."

Steve broke out in a big smile. "Oh. Liz. You don't know how happy this makes me. I am on my way in to meet with the board to give them my answer. I had planned to take the position even before knowing how you felt about me. I prayed last night for an answer. My first request to God, was that you would give us a chance and my second request was that the board would honor what I was asking for in pay. This morning, they called, and they are giving me more than what I asked for and now you are here. Yes, God is good. He just put a seal on what I am to do."

They both hugged and they both felt God had his arms around them, too.

"I'll call you later for I need to get to my meeting. Liz, thank you for coming by this morning." Steve leaned over and kissed her on the forehead.

As Steve walked away, Liz knew that things were going to be alright. Not only had she been praying, but Steve had been praying also, and God heard both prayers. Liz wondered how many people had been praying for them, for she thought about what Jana had said that morning. Then she thought about the women in her shelter. What a testimony she had to share with them. Yes, God's ways were always the right way, and how He could use a situation to bless so many.

Twenty-One

Steve finally got moved to Nashville. Martin Wynn, a doctor, Steve had met when he was interviewing for the position at Vanderbilt, had rented an apartment till he could find a house for his family. Martin asked Steve if he would like to move in with him. It had two bedrooms, they were small, but Martin didn't want anything big, since he would hopefully be moving soon. It was within walking distance to the hospital, so he could walk to work, weather permitting. Steve took him up on the offer.

Steve had only been there three months when Martin came in one day and said, "Great news, my man. Found a house and my wife approved it. We did a video walk-through and she was pleased, so I put a down payment on it and she should be moving here next month. Soon this place will be all yours."

"Take your time, Martin. You have been so gracious in letting me move in here. It's in a great location and the rent isn't so bad. So where did you find a place?"

"It will be a little drive for me, but it's out of the city. This was the fourth video walk-through we had done. She found fault with ever house I showed her. But you know what they say, 'If mama isn't happy, nobody is happy.' Then she said she loved this one, I gave the realtor money right then. It's in a nice neighborhood, so when the baby gets here, it will be a great place for him to grow up in."

"Hey, you didn't tell me it was a boy. When did you find out?"

"When we did the walk-through. She had just left the doctor's office."

"Well, congratulations. A new home and a son on the way. What more could you ask for? Say, when you're ready to move, let me know and I'll help."

"Thanks, Steve. As you can see, I won't be taking much from here and my wife moved in with her parents when I came to Nashville. We didn't have that much, and she sold most of what we had. We thought once we found a place, we would buy furniture that would fit the house."

"Smart thinking, Martin. You said she is in Indiana now?"

"Yeah, that's where her parents live."

"How did you two meet?" Steve asked.

"My sister met her in college. They were roommates and became good friends. She brought her home one summer and I happened to be in on a break myself. She stole my heart, and the rest is history. My sister has been hoping for a girl and asked if we would name the baby after her."

"So, what is your sister's name?"

Laughing, Martin said, "Greta Jane. Don't think a boy would appreciate either name. I know I wouldn't."

"True. Well, if you decide to have another one, maybe it will be a girl."

"Come on, Steve. Let's see how things go with this one before we start planning on another one."

Steve had managed to see Liz only three times since he had move to Nashville. They talked every day, but when one was free, the other one was at work. They both had terrible schedules.

Thanksgiving was fast approaching. Scott and Millie were planning on coming in. Liz and Steve were working on clearing their schedules so they could spend time with them when they came.

Two days before Thanksgiving, Steve text Liz. "What is your schedule for tonight?"

Checking with Dee, Liz realized she was actually free. Steve texted her back to meet him at Kayne Prime Steakhouse. He would like to spend some time with her before Scott and Millie came in, for he knew Millie would commandeer all of Liz's time. He would make reservations for them at six.

On Thanksgiving Day, Liz helped at her house, preparing food for the ladies there. Several from the church had volunteered to help and soon, the lunch meal was ready. She wasn't to be at her parents' home till later that afternoon. Steve texted her that he would stop by and pick her up, and that Scott and Millie had made it in.

When they arrived at Liz's parents, everyone was there. The aroma from all the food filled the house. When the table was set and all were seated, Ryan stood to say the blessing. Before he did, he said, "It is so good to see this table not only full of food, but to see all the family gathered around. This is such a blessing."

Before he said anything else, Steve stood and said, "Mr. Barnett, I don't mean to interrupt, but before you go on, I would like to ask, with your permission, may I have your blessing on asking for your daughter's hand in marriage?"

Dana gasped and put her hand to her mouth. Tears filled her eyes. Ryan looked at Steve, fighting back his own tears. "Absolutely, Dana and I have been waiting for a long time for a son, and God is blessing us with a perfect one. Welcome to the family."

Ryan walked around to hug Steve and Liz. Dana tried get up out of her chair, tears flowing by now. "Oh, I couldn't be happier."

When everyone had said their congratulations and they were all seated again, Liz held out her hand and there was a beautiful diamond ring. Steve had given it to her on the night they had went to Kayne's to eat. Everyone was getting up again only this time to see the ring and give them more hugs.

Smiling, Steve looked at Ryan. "If you hadn't given your blessings, Liz said she would give the ring back to me. I'm so glad you approve, Mr. Barnett."

Ryan looked very seriously at Steve. "Let's get one thing straight, young man. You will not refer to me as Mr. Barnett. You are to call me Dad, just like Liz, and for Dana, you will call her Mom. You are family and that's the way it is around here. Now, before the food is completely cold, let's bless it."

After the meal, Dana and Debbie were in the kitchen discussing wedding plans. Liz walked in with Millie. "Mom, this is my wedding, don't you think I should be the one making the plans?"

Dana turned to Liz. "Yes, of course, dear, but there are some things that Debbie and I want to do. You are our only child, and not just any ole wedding will do. As we decided on things, we will run it by you for your approval.”

“Mom, Steve, and I are going to elope. This will keep things so much simpler.”

Dana’s eye opened wide. “Over my dead body. Since the day you were born, I have looked forward to your wedding day. Don’t you even think of doing such a thing.”

Liz broke out in a laugh and so did Millie. “Mom, I was only joking with you. We have no intentions of eloping. I just wanted to see what you would say.”

Not seeing the humor in Liz’s joke, Dana finally composed herself. Debbie looked at Liz. “That was mean of you, Liz. I was ready to flog you myself if you two eloped.”

“Aunt Debbie, I know how you two sisters are. I don’t think Steve and I could get far enough away from you two if we did that.”

Leaving Dana and Debbie in the kitchen, Liz and Millie went outside. Millie was still laughing at what Liz had done. “You know, what you just did brought back so many memories of things we use to pull on them. Oh, those were some good days.”

“You know Millie, if you and Scott were to move here to Nashville, we could have more of those fun times.”

“Yeah, but Scott hasn’t gotten an offer for a job like Steve. Scott right now is a family doctor, where Steve is a specialist. Big difference in job openings.”

“If he was offered a position here, do you think he would take it? Would you want to move back here?” Liz asked.

“I think about it sometimes. Scott has a really good practice and starting over in another state, I don’t know.”

"Millie, I'm sure with the church, we could build Scott's practice up quickly. You know how well the church likes to support their own, and with word of mouth, he could do very well here."

"We will see. I know I heard him talking to Steve about it. They are close and who knows."

"Millie, remember how close we use to be? It's worth praying about it."

"Ditto."

Twenty-Two

A June wedding was planned and before Liz knew it, June had arrived. Her mom and Aunt Debbie fussed and fussed over how things were to be. Liz had finally given up and told them whatever they wanted was fine with her. Liz called Millie one night and told her about how the two sisters were planning her wedding. Millie laughed, "And you want us to move to Nashville. You do realize that as soon as you and Steve are married, they are going to start asking about when you're going to have a baby?"

"Who is thinking about having a baby? Are you and Scott going to have one?"

"No. But every time I talk to Mom or Dad they hint around about needing a grandbaby. Just letting you know what's ahead."

"Millie, if you and Scott had a baby, Uncle Roy and Aunt Debbie may move to Raleigh!"

"Liz, sometimes, you could keep your thoughts to yourself."

"Just think about it. Look at how they are going on about this wedding. By the way, thanks to you I now have two moms planning my wedding, not just one, but anyway, if you and Scott had a baby, you wouldn't have to worry about setting up a nursery. You would come home one day and there it would be, everything you could possibly want or could think of. Also, you wouldn't have to worry about a babysitter."

"Liz, again, do keep your thoughts to yourself. We are not planning on having a baby any time soon, I was just trying to give you a heads up on what to expect after the wedding. Oh, we will be coming in next Wednesday. I have my dress and Scott will have his tux."

"How many phone calls have you had over your dress, Millie?"

"Honestly Liz, between our moms, you would have thought I knew nothing about dresses or shoes."

"Now you know how I feel. I love them both dearly, but eloping really would have been the best thing we could have done. They showed up one evening at the house and wanted to see if we needed anything. We had a wall knocked down and remodeled my living area so Steve could have his own closet and a desk, plus a few other things. I finally had to set my foot down. I told them the wedding was one thing, but here it was up to Steve and me. This was not only our home, but other people lived here, and I didn't want our area all fancy and the rest of the place ho-hum."

"How did that go?" Millie asked.

"Strangely enough, they backed off, said they thought that made sense. But full speed ahead on the wedding."

"Liz, you can handle them, and I do wish you and Steve the best. If Steve makes you as happy as Scott has made me, you are going to have a wonderful marriage. See you next week."

After hanging up, Liz looked around the room. It was different than it was a month ago. Much bigger and Steve had already moved most of his things in. He was still staying at his apartment until after the wedding. She couldn't believe it, next week she would be married, her life getting ready to take on a new chapter. Liz had wanted to have an outdoor wedding, but her mom and Aunt Debbie would not hear of it. This had to be a church wedding.

The wedding day finally arrived. Liz was trying so hard to keep her sanity, while Dana and Debbie were going at full speed to make sure everything was perfect. As Liz stepped into her dress, she had to admit, it was beautiful. She never dreamed of having a dress like this. As Aunt Debbie fastened the dress she said, "Oh, Liz, inside your dress is a piece of blue material sewn into it. It is part of a dress that our mother wore years ago. Dana and I had saved it and felt it only right you have a little something from your grandmother."

"Oh, Aunt Debbie, that is so thoughtful. I remember my grandmother, although she died when I was young."

Handing Liz her bouquet, Dana said, "Our mama loved peonies, so when we got married, she had peonies in our bouquet. She said it represents a happy marriage and great honor, also pink represents love at first sight. We felt that was the case with you and Steve, you just wouldn't admit it at the time. Anyway, your bouquet has the pink peonies with a blush of ranunculus, which according to the Bible it means the flower of David or the ultimate survivor. Also, we had added a few small yellow roses, which is a symbol of friendship, or 'I love you,' a few purple sweet peas. The purple symbolizes royalty, pride, and success."

"Thank you. It is beautiful. I feel you and Aunt Debbie put a lot of thought in this and it shows. It is perfect."

Dana stepped outside and was gone a good while. Liz turned to Aunt Debbie. "Where is Mom?"

"Helping your dad. He can get dressed by himself, but Dana feels she needs to check him over to make sure everything is exactly as it should be."

Sniggering, Liz said, "I know someone else like that."

Millie walked in and when she saw Liz, she said, "Liz, is this the dress our moms' picked out for you?"

"Is something wrong with it?" both Liz and Debbie asked at the same time.

"No, no, I didn't mean it like that. It's just the dress is so Liz. I was expecting a big frilly dress with a long train, sequins all over it, you know, the whole works."

Debbie said, "That wouldn't be our Liz. At first, Dana and I look at ever so many wedding dresses, all that we like, but for Liz, it wasn't right, so we had to stop and try to think like her, and this is what we came up with."

"Mom, you and Aunt Dana did good. This dress is perfect for her. It's simple, yet elegant. Liz, you look stunning in it."

"Thanks, Millie. For a second, I was afraid something was wrong."

"Wait till Steve sees you. Has Uncle Ryan seen you yet?"

"No, I expect him in here any minute." Liz said.

Millie was filled with so many questions. "Are you nervous? I was when Scott and I married."

"No, not really. It's like when you go to court. You mentally prepare yourself and go for it."

"Liz, can you set aside being an attorney for one day? Try being human."

"Millie, I am being human, and being an attorney comes natural for me, just like taking care of the sick is your thing."

"It just dawned on me. With Steve being a doctor and you an attorney, your poor children are doomed. They don't stand a chance."

"Millie, sometimes the things you come up with amaze me. Have you thought about what kind of children you and Scott might have?"

"Oh, yes. With his brains and my good looks, they will have it made."

Millie laughed and Liz only shook her head. The last thing she want to think about was having kids.

Soon it was time for the wedding to start. The church was decorated beautifully. Dana and Debbie didn't go overboard as they would have liked, trying to keep it the way they thought Liz would have wanted it. At each pew there was a small arrangement of flowers that matched Liz's bouquet. Millie's dress was light pink, and the guys wore a black tux with a burgundy cummerbund. Dana's dress was a different shade of burgundy.

As Ryan walked Liz down the aisle, she noticed a tear in his eye. She squeezed his arm and said, "Daddy, I love you and always will. You and Mama are the best."

When Pastor Rod asked who gives the bride away, as Steve stepped forward to take Liz's hand, he looked at Ryan and said, "I promise to take very good care of her."

Smiling, Ryan replied, "Son, I know you will." Then he gave Liz a kiss. "Your mother and I love you and are so very proud of you." Then a tear rolled down his cheek.

Dana and Debbie had gone all out for the reception. When Liz and Steve walked in, they couldn't believe it. The place was completely decorated and food everywhere. It looked like something you see in a magazine.

Millie walked up to Liz and said, "Now this is more like it. Our moms did this their way. Both girls laughed.

Soon it was time to leave. Liz went to throw her bouquet and Millie said, "Hey, I'm going to sit this one out, I have the man I want." When Liz threw the bouquet, Dee from her office caught it.

Then Steve flipped the garter. It went far in the air and landed on Pastor Rod's plate of food. Looking up, Pastor Rod said, "I can assure you I'm not the next one getting married. Regina and I have been married forty years and counting." Everyone laughed. Steve told him to keep it as a gift from the bride and groom.

As Steve and Liz prepared to leave, everyone was asking where they were going on their honeymoon. Steve said, "Most couples' go to the beach or to some resort, but Liz and I are going to Alaska. We both have always wanted to go and that's what we decided on. We will see everyone in two weeks."

Millie came up to Liz. "You are going to Alaska? Why? And be gone for two weeks? Have you two lost your minds?"

"No, this is something we both decided on. We felt to go that far, we wanted to see as much as we could, so we are taking two weeks."

"Scott and I went to the Bahamas. That's what newlyweds do. You go on trips to Alaska for a second or third honeymoon."

"Millie, are you forgetting something? Steve is a doctor and I'm an attorney. We are expected to do things differently. We are doomed. Remember."

"No, I said your poor children would be doomed and this proves it."

Ryan dropped Liz and Steve off at Liz's till time to go to the airport.

Twenty-Three

Two years had passed since Liz and Steve were married. Dee came in one morning and said,

"Remember when you got married and I caught the bridal bouquet? Well, it took a while, but I'm engaged. Soon I will be getting married."

Liz looked up in total shock. "This is wonderful as long as you don't leave me. You have been with me for so long, I can't imagine having anyone else work for me. Who is the lucky guy?"

"I'm surprised you haven't caught on, for he is in here all the time. It's Drew Jordan." Looking so surprised, Liz said, "Drew! Our Drew here. I know he is in here a lot, but so are other police officers."

"Don't you remember him being at your wedding? We came together. He was so disappointed that he didn't catch the garter and I caught the bouquet."

"Oh yes. The garter went in Pastor Rod's plate. That was so funny."

"Drew tried to catch it, but a row of chairs was between him and where it landed."

"Dee, I am so happy for you, and your ring is beautiful. Knowing you are marrying Drew; now I don't have to worry about losing my secretary. You are my right arm, and I can't possibly do without you."

"Drew has moved up to a lieutenant now. He said he would someday like to be the chief of police but as long as Chief Helton holds that position, it could be a long wait."

"It may be a really long wait, for I can't see him giving that up, but I am happy for Drew. He is very dedicated to his job, and he takes it very seriously. Tell him not to give up, hang on to that dream."

That evening, Liz received a call from Bill Master. "Liz, my dear, Gloria and I will be in Nashville in about two weeks, and I wanted to make sure you would be home."

"Yes, I will. How are you and Mrs. Master doing?"

"Doing wonderfully. How is your home doing?"

"Oh, it is doing good. I can't tell you how many women we have helped, and some have come with children. You donating this building was a blessing we will never forget. The location, the size of the place is perfect. The people from the church have poured so many loving hours here, even other churches have wanted to help."

"Liz, God made it possible for you to have that building. He has also blessed my family so much and continues to do so. Take care and we will see you in two weeks."

Liz was eager for Steve to meet Bill and Gloria Master. She and Millie had talked about Master Department Store so much. On the day of their arrival, Liz and Steve had taken the day off from work. When they walked in, Liz thought, they haven't aged at all. They looked the same as when they gave her the building. Liz introduced them to Steve, then took them around to show them all they had done and how they had expanded her living area to make room for Steve. They seemed so happy to meet him.

After lunch, Liz asked them how things were going in Florida and with their family.

"That's why we are here, Liz." said Bill Master. "We have something to tell you. It's about this place."

Liz wasn't sure what to expect. She looked at Steve and then back at the Masters. Her first thought was, were they going to ask for the building back? Maybe they wanted to come back and run the place. So many things went through Liz's mind.

Bill Master cleared his throat and then looked at his watch. He nodded his head at his wife, and she took out her phone and text something. Then he looked back at Liz and Steve.

"It always amazes me at how God works. He always has a plan and if we listen to Him, those plans work out beautifully." Tears came into his eyes. "You see, many years ago, one of our daughters met a man, whom we disapproved of. Nothing we said seemed to help. Then one day, she left with him, and we haven't heard from her since. We tried everything we could to find her, but it was like she had vanished. Gloria and I have never stopped praying for her. We felt God would let us know what happened or He would hopefully bring her back to us and He did. Like I said, God always has a plan, and we must be obedient."

While they were talking, Gill walked in, "Excuse me, Liz, I don't mean to interrupt, but you have some visitors."

In walked Beth McCloud and Joanna. Liz and Steve both got up and went to them. "This is a surprise," Liz said. "We weren't expecting to see you two today. Come I want you to meet someone. This is Bill and Gloria Master."

Bill Master stood up. "Liz, Beth McCloud is our daughter. She lives in Kentucky. She and her husband, Kenneth, operate Master's store there."

Steve and Liz stood frozen, not sure what to say. Finally, Steve spoke up. "We had no idea that Beth was related to you."

Bill Master motioned, "Please, let's all sit down. I know this is a surprise, but remember God's hand is always at work. When we gave Liz this place, we had no idea a child would be dropped off at her doorstep. Apparently, the person who dropped Joanna off wanted her to be at a safe place, at least this is what we want to think. According to Joanna, Liz was there for her and went to great lengths to not only protect her, but to reassure her that God was with her and would help her. Liz planted a very special seed." Bill Master had to stopped and compose himself. Gloria took her hand and placed it on his. She only smiled, as a tear formed in her own eye.

Clearing his throat again, he went on, "When Joanna was sent to Raleigh, there she was given to a young doctor that specialized in coma patients. We feel through Dr. Steve Hunter's knowledge, through many prayers, and God's love, the child pulled through. Beth and Kenneth had decided they wanted another child, and they heard about Joanna. Most of the time when you try to adopt, a lot of legal things get in the way and takes a lot of time, but this wasn't the case here. It went through so easily. Beth and Kenneth were delighted to have a daughter in their home. Joanna is a very bright and loving person. She had no problem adjusting to us and we felt she was truly one of us from the very beginning when we met. As you know, she wanted to go into the medical field, which is what she is doing. She went to Lake Cumberland Regional Hospital to do some clinicals. One day she walked in on a patient that was very sick. His health was failing him, and he had trouble seeing. According to his records, he had no family. When Joanna walked closer to the man, she recognized him. He was her biological father. As she stood there, her memory started coming back to her. She turned, left the room, and called Beth. Kenneth and Beth both went to her. The next week was a very bad week for her as her memory returned. She was able to recall all the beatings she had gone through. It seems the child could do nothing right for the man. As for her mother, all she remembers is that her parents left one evening, and she was told to stay in bed while they were gone. The next morning, she was told her mother had left and would not be back. Joanna was about nine when her mother left."

Bill Master stopped talking and looked at Joanna. A smile came across his face, then tears rolled down his cheek. Gloria, Beth, Kenneth, and Joanna all had tears. Liz and Steve sat in silence, not sure what to say.

Taking a deep breath, Bill Master began speaking again. He looked at Liz and Steve and said, "If this building had been our department store, Joanna would not have been dropped off here. God laid it on our hearts to give this building to you, and we are so glad we did. You see, our daughter, Brooke, left home to married Clarence Walters. Joanna is our granddaughter."

Liz felt like the floor would swallow her up. She could not control her tears. She couldn't believe what she was hearing. Joanna was Bill and Gloria Masters' grandchild and Beth was her aunt. No one said anything for a few minutes. Steve and Liz, trying hard to absorb all that they had just heard, looked at first one person, then another.

Finally, Bill Master spoke. "Remember I said God had a plan. We never dreamed we had a grandchild, by Brooke. Only God could work all this out. We hate that the child had to suffer like she did, but being dropped off at your doorstep, then sent to Raleigh to be healed, only for a pastor to make it known about a child needing a home, then Beth and Kenneth deciding they wanted to adopt. God brought this all full circle. He brought our grandchild to our store where she would find her way to us."

Liz looked at Beth. "Did you know Joanna was your niece?"

"No, we didn't know Brooke even had a child. Like Daddy said, at times, Joanna seemed like a blood family member, not one that was adopted."

Joanna finally spoke. "When I went to Kentucky to live, I never felt I was among strangers. When we went to Florida to visit, I was even comfortable with them. Everyone was so easy to love, I felt like I was one of them. It's really hard to explain."

Steve asked. "Do you remember what your birth name was?"

"They called me Carrie, that's all that I remember."

Liz immediately thought of what Chief Helton had told her. They had thought then that Joanna was possibly Carrie, but they didn't have concrete proof.

Beth took a seat by Liz. "When Joanna's memory returned, we sent off for her birth certificate. We wanted to change her name to McCord and find out any other information that we could." Reaching inside her purse, she pulled out an envelope and handed it to Liz. "You need to read this."

As Liz took the paper out of the envelope and unfolded it, in her hand was Joanna's birth certificate when she was born. Her parents had named her Carrie Joanna Master. Liz looked up.

"I had no idea. A friend of mine in college, her name was Joanna. While I was praying about a name for her, I remembered my friend's name. She had told me her name meant 'God is gracious.'

Bill Master said, "Liz, God is gracious."

Steve reached out to put his arm around Liz, she turned and fell into his arms crying. Not a dry eye could be found in the room. Tears flowing everywhere, but they were tears of happiness and rejoicing in God's wonderful goodness.

Gloria, spoke up. "Bill's mother's first name was Carrie, my mother's first name was Anna, and my middle name is Jo. If you notice on the birth certificate, Brooke's last name was still Master, and the child is listed as Carrie Joanna Master. It does list the father as Clarence Walters. From what we can find out, Brooke never married Clarence, and Carrie's last name stayed Master on her birth certificate."

Liz realized then, why they had not been able to find a birth certificate for Joanna. They were searching for Carrie Walters.

As everyone began to pull themselves together, Steve turned to Joanna. "I hope you don't mind me asking, but did you ever go and talk to your dad?"

Joanna dropped her head for a minute then said. "Yes. It took me a while, but through much praying, I finally decided I needed to see him and try to talk to him. I went by myself, I told no one I was going. When I walked into his room, due to his poor eyesight, he didn't know who I was. When I told him, he sat very still, never moved or said anything. I told him I remember that night. I told him due to the beating, it had taken a very long time for my body to heal and mend itself, but I had made a full recovery due to so many loving people caring for me, so many prayers and by God's healing hands. I explained my memory had not returned till I saw him and then it all came back. I told him about my move to North Carolina, the adoption and finding my family. My mother's family. Still, he never moved or said a word. Then I told him, I was so grateful that he had dropped me off at the place he did. I explained that it was once my grandparent's department store and that my mother had grown up there as a little girl. I know he didn't know it at the time, but he had taken me home to find my family. I reached over and laid my hand on his and told him I forgave him for what he did. I reminded him of some scripture in the Bible in Luke 23:34, where it says, *'Father, forgive them, for they do not know what they are doing.'* Also, in I Corinthians 13:4, it states in that verse, *'that love keeps no records of wrongs.'* I also explained that in Ephesians 4: 31-32, it says, *'Get rid of all bitterness, rage, and anger, brawling and slander, along with every form of malice. Be kind and compassionate to one another, forgiving each other, just as in Christ God forgave you.'* As I stood to leave, I look back at him, and I saw tears running down his face. I never said any more, I left. Two days later, I found out he passed away."

Beth spoke up. "We were surprised that Joanna went to see him, but after she told us, we feel she did the right thing. She is a very strong and brave woman, whom we are so proud of."

"If I may add one thing more," Joanna said. "Before I went to see him, as I was praying, I remembered Liz praying over me many times. Several of her prayers and readings I recall. I know one day, she read to me Ephesians 4:31-32. She told me once I did this, I would start healing within. I didn't understand at first, but she read that and many other scriptures over and over to me. Another one she read that stayed with me was Matthew 22:37-39. *'Love the Lord your God with all your heart and with all your soul and with all your mind. This is the first and greatest commandment. And the second is like it: Love your neighbor as yourself.'* You see I could hear, but I couldn't respond. So, as I laid there, I repeated in my mind what she prayed and read to me. No one had ever mentioned the Bible to me, and I found it soothing and peaceful. It helped me to heal in many ways. That's why, Liz, you will always be very special to me. I needed that when I first went to the hospital. When they sent me to Duke, I missed you very much, then Pastor Felty came to visit, then Dr. Hunter, and both loved the Bible and God. Everything I went through; God was making a way for me to be with my family. It took a while, but it was worth it. Christ died on the cross for us, and to Him it was worth it."

Liz rose and went to Joanna. "I am so proud of you and who you have become."

At the end of the day, when everyone had left, Liz walked outside and looked up at the sign over the door. While she was standing there, Bill Master walked up to her.

"Gloria and I have been sitting over there in the car looking at this building. For many years, it read 'Master's Department Store.' Seeing your sign touches our hearts so much more, not because it has the name Master on it, for we don't see it as our last name, we see it as our heavenly Master. Liz, you couldn't have given this place a more perfect name, for it is truly a place of love. 'LOVE BY THE MASTER.'

Books by

Vicki M. Irwin

A Journey for Rebecca

By Grace

Love By The Master

Love is patient, love is kind.

It does not envy, it does not boast,

It is not proud.

It is not rude, it is not self-seeking,

It is not easily angered,

It keeps no records of wrongs.

Love does not delight in evil but

Rejoices with the truth.

It always protects, always trust,

always hopes, always perseveres.

Love never fails.

I Corinthians 13:4-8
(NIV)

About the Author

Vicki McBee Irwin was born in Maryville, Tennessee. She married her high school sweetheart, Larry. They have three children, nine grandchildren, and ten great grandchildren. With her husband's Air Force career, Vicki has been blessed to travel to all fifty states and many places abroad. To this day, Vicki and Larry love to travel and enjoy seeing all the many beautiful places God has created. Besides writing and traveling, Vicki also enjoys scrapbooking, sewing, cooking, playing the piano, and, of course, spending time with her family.

If you enjoyed this story, please help Vicki encourage others to read it by writing a review. No matter where you purchased the book, you can post a review on social media, Amazon.com, and elsewhere. On behalf of all authors, and readers, thank you!